Hannah
Stands Tall

Hannah Stands Tall

by

Shirley Rees

BONNEVILLE BOOKS™
Springville, Utah

ISBN: 1-55517-652-6
v.1

Published by Bonneville Books
Imprint of Cedar Fort Inc.
www.cedarfort.com

Distributed by:

Typeset by Kristin Nelson
Cover design by Adam Ford
Cover design © 2002 by Lyle Mortimer

Printed in the United States of America
10 9 8 7 6 5 4 3 2 1

Printed on acid-free paper

Library of Congress Cataloging-in-Publication Data

Rees, Shirley.
  Hannah stands tall / by Shirley Rees.
     p. cm.
Summary: After Hannah's mother dies, the fifteen-year-old assumes the tasks of taking care of her siblings and helping her father on their southern Utah farm.
  ISBN 1-55517-652-6 (alk. paper)
  [1. Frontier and pioneer life--Utah--Fiction. 2. Farm life--Utah--Fiction. 3. Utah--History--19th century--Fiction.] I. Title.
  PZ7.R25493 Han 2002
  [Fic]--dc21
                        2002008037

To my students of Holdaway Elementary,
whose love of literature inspired me to write.

And to my Aunt Ruth, who compiled stories
of our ancestors in Southern Utah.

Chapter 1

Dreary. That's what it was. Hovering gray clouds deepened the February dusk, and even though the cabin glowed in the light of an oil lamp, and the wood stove provided warmth, dreary was how I felt. Should have been a pleasant time, logs crackling, the mingled aroma of a wood fire and simmering chicken stew, but without Ma's smiling face and cheerful voice, my heart was as gray as those clouds.

Nellie, eleven, three years younger than I, let go of the churn paddle and stretched. "Feels like the butter's turned, and about time. My arms are like to fall off. Want me to throw another log in the stove?"

I nodded. "Just a small one. Don't want to burn the biscuits." I gave the stew a stir, blew on the wooden spoon, and sampled the gravy. "Ought to satisfy Pa. It's a far sight better than the noodle soup."

"Let's hope so," said Nellie.

"It wasn't that bad. Just a mite salty."

Nellie turned to me and smiled. "How could you know what a generous sprinkle meant? You were just a sight more generous than Ma."

Thank goodness for Nellie. Her spirits never sagged for long. Ma said she was born smiling. Now she shouldered her share of the work without complaining. She was small-boned, slender, and pretty with her blonde hair, green eyes, and a sprinkle of freckles across her nose. How could sisters be so different? Folks spoke of me as the "tall, sturdy, red-headed one with brown eyes like her pa's."

Contemplating the unfairness of life, I kneaded the soft

dough, pinched off round biscuits, arranged them on the cast iron pan, and slipped them into the oven—Ma's oven. The stove was her pride and joy. And I must say, Ma was not a prideful woman. As I closed the oven and wiped the flour off my hands, the cabin door flew open with a bang. Five-year-old Willy burst in followed by Ruff, tracking mud across the kitchen, over-turning the churn, and spilling its contents across the floor.

"*Willy, get that dog . . .*" I stopped when I saw the fear in my little brother's eyes, and my stomach took a sickening dive.

"The gun, Hannah! Get the gun! A mountain lion! It's after the sheep. Caleb needs the gun!"

I could scarcely hear him for Ruff's frantic barking. With rust fur bristling, he leaped about the kitchen colliding with Willy who slipped, landing in a mixture of mud and buttermilk. Tears streamed down his cheeks. "You better hurry, Hannah," he wailed.

I looked at Willy, sitting in the middle of that greasy puddle, and didn't know whether to laugh or cry, so I grabbed the gun and ran toward the sheep pen. Nellie and Willy followed, while Ruff, a safe distance behind, growled menac-ingly. "Cowardly dog," I mumbled. "Should be out there protecting the sheep."

Caleb stood just outside the pen yelling as he hurled rocks at a shadow crouched in the bushes twenty yards away. Good thing Ma couldn't hear the words he was using. Pa either, for that matter.

Caleb was small for his age, but fierce in defending our farm. Thunder rumbled in the distance, and sheet lightning lit up the western horizon. The lion snarled, sending Ruff into a fit of frenzied barking.

"Quick, gimme the gun!" Caleb's words rang with urgency.

Ignoring him, I stepped forward, shouldered the rifle and took aim at the lion. Pa's words echoed in my head. "Now that your Ma's gone, I'm depending on you to take care of things." I wasn't about to give Caleb the gun. With heart pounding, I steadied my trembling hands, tightened my finger on the trigger, and adjusted the aim. I found myself staring into the glowing eyes of the tawny cat and knew I couldn't kill him. I couldn't abide more death. As I raised the rifle and fired, the stock slammed against my shoulder sending me staggering backwards. With a scream, the lion turned and bounded into the brush.

"Did ya get him, Hannah?" Willy was on his way to the shadowy spot where the lion had crouched, but Nellie grabbed his arm. Peering into the bushes, he asked, "Can we skin 'im?"

"Not likely." Caleb didn't hide his scorn. "I don't think that old lion'd stand still for it—if we could catch him." He glared at me with his brown eyes flashing. He pushed his dark hair off his forehead, turned angrily about, and proceeded to herd the sheep into the shed.

My face burned with shame. Caleb had been acting too big for his britches lately, and I wasn't about to explain my actions to him. It was easier to let him think that fear had spoiled my aim. He was sure to have plenty to say about that. Considering how I regularly whipped him at target shooting, he'd be mighty happy to report how I'd missed when it counted.

Twilight was fading as I stalked across the barnyard with Nellie at my heels. As we came in sight of the cabin, acrid smoke billowed out of the open door carrying with it an unmistakable odor. "Oh, no!" said Nellie, as we broke into a run. "No biscuits tonight."

Pa arrived to find us on our knees mopping up butter and mud while wisps of smoke wafted near the ceiling. He stared and shook his head. "There must be a right interesting explanation for this." I looked up and must have been a sorry sight, for he only added, "I'll not track up your floor. Call when dinner's ready." Then he walked out the door and turned toward the barn. Caleb and Willy would make sure he heard about my failure as a protector of the family's livestock.

My shoulder throbbed where the gun stock had pounded it. The rough wood-slab floor had scraped and gouged my knuckles. I sat back and plucked at a splinter. It wasn't fair. On top of everything, I'd doubtless end up on the wrong end of a scolding. "Oh, Ma, I miss you so." A tear of self-pity threatened to spill down my cheek. I glanced over at Nellie, dutifully mopping away, then peered down at the filthy mop cloth in my hands. I found some small comfort in the fact that we'd not have to turn *these* old rags into a rug or quilt.

An hour later, the floor was mopped, the table set, and the butter that had remained in the churn was salvaged. Lacking biscuits, we could use it on the corn cake left from breakfast. Light from a lantern bobbed toward the house. Then the pump squeaked and splashed as Pa and the boys washed up. A brisk wind blew across the room as they came in. "Close the door and wipe your feet!" I ordered. I expected a rebuke for my rudeness, but Pa just raised his dark eyebrows and wiped his shoes.

"She gives orders a mite better than she shoots," said Caleb as he scuffed his boots on the old rag rug by the door. "That mountain cat weren't more than ten yards away. Shot went right over his head."

"Caleb could've killed that ol' lion, couldn't ya, Caleb? He wouldn't get away from you." Willy aimed his arm. "*Pow! Pow!*"

"We'll have no more of that. Hang up your coats," ordered Pa. "Smells like dinner's ready."

Caleb sniffed. "Smells like burned biscuits to me." A look from Pa put an end to Caleb's remarks.

I brought the steaming stew to the table and ladled it into earthenware bowls. Then we knelt for the blessing. Pa's deep voice resonated in the room. "Our most gracious Lord, we kneel to thank thee for our many blessings—"

At that, something inside me exploded. Anger, sorrow--I didn't know what. I jumped from the table, sending the chair clattering across the floor. As I stumbled up the stairs to the loft, my eyes burned, but no tears came. I flopped onto the bed I shared with Nellie and buried my face in the rough muslin pillow cover.

Minutes later the stairs creaked under Pa's weight. He said nothing, just sat on the chair beside my bed. When his hand touched my shoulder, I thought to ignore him, but instead, turned over and looked into his sad, brown eyes. If only I could throw my arms around his neck the way I used to and feel his rough beard against my cheek, but something held me back.

"All our blessings, Pa? What blessings? Ma and Jenny are dead! Why would God take a little thing like Jenny, barely three? And Grandma York and Sally Richmond, buried somewhere along the wagon trail. Grandpa York, killed at Haun's Mill. Blessings, Pa?" I couldn't stop. The words just tumbled out. "The weather, the land, everything is against us. God's forgotten us out here in this forsaken place."

Pa shook his head. "No, God hasn't forgotten us. We don't always understand his ways, but we mustn't fail to acknowledge our blessings. You have to remember, death is only a temporary parting. God knows each of us. He never gives a person more trials than he's able to bear."

"He must not know me, Pa."

"It's been a bad day for you. Come eat. The stew is hot and filling." He stood as if to go, then turned back. "You're good with the rifle, Hannah. Seems strange you would miss."

"I saw his eyes. I couldn't kill him."

"Then you should have let Caleb do it. The cat will likely come back." With that quiet rebuke, he left.

A bad day? There hadn't been a good day since Ma and Jenny came down sick with diphtheria. How could Pa talk about blessings? I wiped away a tear before it could roll down my cheek. Temporary parting? Ma would be gone for the rest of my life.

I didn't want to go downstairs and hear how ungrateful I was and how thankful I should be. And I certainly didn't want to hear Caleb's taunts about my shooting. Then again, my stomach felt hollow, and I realized it would be a long time till breakfast. Hunger won out. I swallowed my pride and started down the narrow stairs.

Hot and filling indeed! Was that all he could say about my stew?

Chapter 2

As the night wore on, rain continued to drum on the roof while wind rattled windows and seeped through invisible cracks. The wood stove warmed the kitchen, but the rest of the house grew damp and cold. I found myself wishing Pa hadn't brought us south to this remote spot in the Utah Territory. After chores were finished, we gathered around the warmth of the wood fire, and by the light of a flickering oil lamp, Pa read from the scriptures.

I guess he had warned the boys before I came down, for there was no mention of the mountain lion. Must have been just about more than Caleb could endure, since of late, he delighted in reminding me of my shortcomings. At twelve, he was a head shorter than I, a condition that he found most annoying. I hoped he would soon shoot up a foot and pass me by. That might make him a sight easier to live with. Lying on the hearth rug next to Willy, he fidgeted and yawned while Pa read.

Finally Pa closed the book. "Best we prepare for bed. It's been a right busy day."

"It's cold upstairs," complained Willy.

"I've put the warming stones in the oven," I told him. "You can help me wrap them. Wouldn't want your toes to freeze. You'd be wanting to get in my bed to warm them on my back."

I took the heated rocks out of the oven, and we wrapped them in rags. Pa banked the fire while Caleb brought in a load of wood. Then I lit a candle, and the four of us headed up the stairs, foot-warmers in hand, while Pa retired to his room—the room I'd always thought of till now as Ma's room.

Halfway up the stairs, Caleb blurted, "Next time ya better leave the shootin' to me, see'n as how when it matters, you can't hit the broad side of a barn."

I knew he couldn't let it be. Couldn't hardly wait till Pa was out of earshot. I ignored him—something he couldn't stand—and led Willy to his bed under the eaves in the corner of the room I shared with Nellie. He'd been sleeping there since Ma died. Pa depended on me to comfort Willy when he woke up crying.

"Don't see why I can't sleep in Caleb's room," he complained.

"'Cause if you needed something, can't anything wake Caleb," I said.

Nellie tucked a hot stone under his covers. "Course, if the roof fell in, that might rouse him."

"And Caleb wouldn't like jumping out of bed to bring you the chamber pot," I reminded him. "Besides, we need you in here in case there's a mouse to catch. Can't Nellie or me stand to touch 'em." I tucked him in, brushed back a tangle of red curls, and kissed him on the forehead.

"An ol' mouse come around, I'll get 'im," Willy boasted. "I been wanting me a pet." He snuggled under the quilts, and within minutes his eyes were closed. Perhaps tonight he wouldn't wake up crying for Ma.

I slipped into my flannel nightgown, blew out the candle, and dived under the covers next to Nellie, stretching my foot toward the welcome warmth of the heated stone. We lay for awhile in silence, listening to the rain beat a steady rhythm on the roof.

Then she reached out and touched my shoulder. "Hannah? I don't like it when you and Pa fight." Her voice was soft, barely audible.

"We're not fighting," I answered. "I just don't understand

him anymore. How can he talk about blessings? Grandpa and Grandma York dead. Then Ma. It's like he's forgotten that she's gone. Just expects everything to go on same as before with me taking over the house chores."

"I'll help you."

I sighed. "I know. It's not the work. But sometimes he acts like Ma dying is just another setback—like the flood washing away part of his alfalfa."

"Hannah, that's a terrible thing to say! Pa loved Ma."

Her voice quavered, and I could hear the hurt. Nellie didn't need me heaping more sorrow on her. I hugged her skinny frame. "Don't pay me any mind. Like Pa said, it's been a bad day."

I lay in the dark, unable to sleep. It *had* been a bad day. But it was more than that. There had been a lot of bad days since Ma and Jenny took sick with diphtheria. If Pa hadn't brought us to this remote spot, Ma might be alive. If the doctor had been closer and able to get here sooner, he might have saved them. If only I had been able to help, but Pa had kept me away. Said he didn't want the rest of us coming down sick. So many ifs. And I never did see Pa shed a tear. Not when they died. Not at the burying. And not once since then. He put Ma's picture away in a trunk and went on with life—thanking God for our blessings.

I tossed about on our straw mattress, earning a mumbled complaint from Nellie. Finally I fell into a troubled sleep where shadows concealed dark, ominous secrets—where glowing yellow eyes stared at me. Then from somewhere in the shadows came a whisper. "Hannah, Hannah." It was Ma calling me. I turned toward the comfort of her voice, but it faded away and was gone.

Then I was running through a field, pursued by a snarling lion. A driving rain beat against me. My feet were heavy, *so heavy*, as I struggled to lift them out of the muddy quagmire. A gun hung at my side, but my arms were too weak to lift it. Pa's voice was echoing in my head. "Should have shot him. He'll be back. He'll be back."

Then the dream changed. I was no longer in the field, but standing beside a churning stream, surrounded by the sound of the rushing torrent. Gripped by fear, I wanted to run, but my legs wouldn't move. Then a small girl walked to the bank and stood tottering there. I reached out, but she tumbled slowly over the edge and disappeared under the foaming water. I called for Ma, but when I turned around there was no one there, just a wooden coffin by a newly-dug grave.

I woke with a start, grabbing Nellie, who mumbled something and turned over.

I lay shaking, but not from cold. Lightning illuminated the room as thunder rumbled across the sky. I didn't want to go back to sleep, didn't want to slip back into that familiar nightmare—the nightmare that brought with it memories of a day by the bank of the Platte River when I was five—memories I wanted to forget. Sally Richmond had died. She was my best friend. Now, fear of the water lay hidden in a crevice of my mind, creeping out at night into my dreams, turning me into a coward.

I eased out of bed, crept to the window, and looked out into the black night. Through the rain, I could see the dark outline of cottonwoods that lined the Santa Rosa Creek. The water would be rising, sweeping branches and logs along in the muddy torrent. I shuddered. It was too much like that other river. As I stood there shivering in the cold, I remembered the gentle sound of Ma's voice calling my name. A tear rolled down my cheek.

I was about to go back to bed when something moved on the path by the fence, sending my heart to racing. The dream had put me in a mind to jump at every shadow. Probably just Ruff, I told myself. Silly dog ought to be under the porch out of the rain. As another flash of lightning brought the yard into view, I saw a man wearing a slicker. I stared, afraid to move, but as the figure drew closer, relief swept over me. It was Pa. But what was he doing out in the rain? Had the mountain lion returned? Maybe all the noise wasn't thunder. Hard to tell if there had been a gun shot, what with the storm raging, but I could see no gun. Didn't seem Pa'd go out at this hour to check on the animals, and he wasn't coming from the direction of the barn.

I hesitated at the top of the stairs wondering whether to go down. The hinges squeaked as the door opened. Then the bolt was eased carefully into place. The floor creaked, but no light came from below. I heard Pa's door close and decided I might as well go back to bed. It seemed he hadn't wanted to wake us. It was silly of me to worry, but the question still nagged at me. What was Pa doing out in the rain?

Chapter 3

Just when I thought we'd never see the sun again, the rain was gone. After three weeks of never-ending downpour, the dark clouds departed leaving wispy white puffs in a blue sky. Friday morning, we awoke to bright rays slanting through the windows. I had a hankering to frolic in the blessed sunshine, so I didn't blame Willy for wanting to dash out and hunt for toads. What with all the mud I'd cleaned up of late, a little more wouldn't matter.

When Pa returned from milking, he said the road was still too muddy for the wagon to make it two miles, let alone the six to Brockton. We'd have to miss church again this week. Though the boys tried, they couldn't hide their pleasure at this pronouncement. They should have known Pa would make sure we observed the Sabbath anyway.

As for me, I looked forward to our weekly trips, for it always included a visit with the Whitlocks. Eliza Whitlock had long been my best friend, and though I'd never let on, especially to Caleb, I looked forward to seeing her brother Charles almost as much. He was sixteen, tall, even taller than I, and had the most fascinating brown eyes flecked with green. Besides, I sure enough wouldn't mind getting away from the farm. But Pa was right, the rough track, only border-line passable when dry, would be near impossible now.

The following days, the sun continued to bless us with its presence. Occasional sprinkles of rain never lasted long. It was about more than I could do to keep the boys' attention on their lessons. Ma had been a school teacher when she married Pa and was determined that we have an education. With no schools near, she had taught us herself. Now, teaching the others was my responsibility. Ma would expect it. The boys had accepted the daily routine of reading and arithmetic when somber gray clouds hemmed us in, but with the spring sun shining through the windows, they resisted my efforts.

"Don't see why I got to sit around here studyin' grammar. Should be out there helping Pa get the grinding wheel fixed. I ain't going to be no English teacher," said Caleb.

"Well, thank providence for that. You'd set English back by quite a piece. It sounds like we've got a good bit of work to do on your grammar. Ma'd be scandalized to hear the way you've been talking of late," I said.

Willy held his slate in front of me. "Can I go now? I done a whole page of my letters. Might not be sunny later."

I gave in. "All right. But you'll have to study hard tomorrow."

So the week went by with study, chores, and mud. No amount of sweeping could keep up with the ever-present red mud. Then finally the ground was dry enough for Pa to work in the fields. He and Caleb left at dawn to replant where the creek had washed away part of the corn crop.

"Don't see why I couldn't go with Pa." Willy sat at the table sulking. "Caleb always gets to help."

Nellie put a bowl of mush in front of him. "When they left, you were sound asleep. Besides, you should be working on catching that mouse."

"Don't think there is an old mouse," he grumped. "Been looking, but I ain't seen 'im."

"Willy, you know you're not supposed to say 'ain't,'" I reminded him. "And there sure enough must be a mouse, 'cause I've seen droppings. Nellie and I have washing and cleaning to do, so finish your breakfast. Then you can feed the chickens and gather the eggs. Unless of course, you'd rather wash the dishes."

I turned to Nellie. "Best we get to work. Seems like there's about as much mud inside as out."

Nellie nodded, looked around the room, and sighed. "Look at Ma's kitchen. She'd about die from shame if she saw it. Couldn't stand a dirty house." Tears dampened her cheeks.

I put an arm around her shoulder. "Then let's get busy and start with the washing. I've set the water on to heat."

Three hours later, clean clothes danced on the line, and sheets billowed in the breeze like sails on a ship. I took a deep breath. "Like Ma always said, isn't anything smells better than clean wash drying in the sun. Almost makes up for my aching back."

"I'm partial to the smell of lilacs myself. Less work, too," said Nellie. "Shouldn't be long till they're blooming."

We sat on the porch, where warmed by the sun and caressed by the breeze, we leaned back enjoying the day. That is until Nellie sat up and looked around. "Wonder where Willy's gone?"

Where was Willy? A sick feeling washed over me. "He brought the eggs in. How long ago was that?" I feared the answer.

"Seems like we were just starting the wash."

Then I remembered. I'd been bending over the wash board struggling with the sheets when he came in, proud of the bucket of eggs he'd found. He'd wanted me to push him in the swing, but I told him he could pump himself. Ashamed of my indifference, I jumped up, and followed by Nellie, ran around the corner of the house to the old mulberry tree. The swing hung there, empty and still.

Trembling, I called, "Willy! Willy York!" No answer came. The only sound was a robin singing in the orchard.

"Like as not, he's down by the barn playing with Ruff," said Nellie.

We raced down the path, ignoring puddles that splattered us with muddy water.

On the far side of the cottonwood trees, the Santa Rosa rushed along with a sound like thunder. I tried to ignore it—fought to erase the picture of the angry water, but I couldn't erase the image of a child tumbling slowly off a river bank.

Tears blurred my vision. "You search in the barn. I'll go over by the creek."

"Don't cry, Hannah. We'll find him. He's likely off hunting squirrels or snakes." I left the path and ran through the brush toward the line of cottonwoods, paying no mind to brambles that tore at my dress and scratched my legs. I was aware only of the sound of water and an overwhelming sense of fear. I came to the edge of the Santa Rosa Creek and ran along the bank calling, afraid I'd find Ruff alone, whining by the rushing stream. A root caught my foot and I sprawled onto the damp ground. I lay there for a moment, then sat up facing the muddy torrent. "Please," I prayed, "don't take Willy, too."

Knowing I had to get help, I raced back toward the path and met Nellie coming from the barnyard. "I'm going for Pa. You stay at the house in case Willy comes home."

I don't know how I was able to run, my body being numb like it was. Must have been fear that kept my legs moving. Why hadn't I watched him? Pa expected me to take care of things at home, expected me to care for Willy. I crossed the bridge and forced myself to peer down at the debris caught on the bridge support, fearful of what I might find. I shook with relief. Nothing but logs and branches.

I ran on down the road, gasping for breath, past the upper pasture, past a field of alfalfa. Then as I drew nearer to the corn field, I heard a familiar sound. A dog was barking. Ruff! "Oh, please, let Willy be with him." I rounded the bend and saw them. Willy, covered with mud, laughed and giggled as he chased Ruff along the far edge of the field.

Fear evaporated. Gasping for breath, I managed to yell, "Willy, get yourself over here right now! I've been hunting all over creation for you!"

As Pa walked toward me, I turned my anger on him. "How long has Willy been here? You let him stay, knowing I'd be sick with worry? Seems you could have sent him home with Caleb."

"I needed Caleb's help. You were to be watching Willy. Hopefully you've learned to be more mindful of your responsibilities." His voice softened. "From the looks of you, the lesson has been hard learned."

I turned away, my face burning with shame and anger. Pa was right. I should have been watching Willy. I knew that without him telling me, but it was cruel to let me worry. He didn't seem to consider the washing, cooking, and cleaning I was expected to do. Ma could handle it all, but I wasn't Ma.

"Hurry up, Willy," I ordered. "We're going home."

"It's about time you came to fetch him. And take Ruff. Those two have been right bothersome," called Caleb.

"Have not. I've been helping. Pa even said so." Willy glared at Caleb, put down his hoe, and walked toward me. I grabbed his arm and marched off up the road. My hair was snarled, my dress was ripped, and I was boiling mad. Willy stumbled behind, struggling to keep up. Ruff ignored us both as he trotted along, exploring the roadside. Willy knew I was angry, but finally he said, "Yer walkin' too fast, Hannah."

I slowed a bit and spoke between clenched teeth. "Nellie's at home, worried sick about you. Best we hurry back and let her know you're all right. Looks as if it may take all afternoon to clean off that mud."

We strode along in silence for a time. Then he said, "Yer hurtin' my arm. Don't be mad. You were busy, so I went to help Pa."

I stopped and looked down at his upturned face with its freckles and deep blue eyes. He hadn't drowned. Tears ran down my cheeks. I knelt down and put my hands on his shoulders. "Don't ever run off like that again," I whispered. "You about scared the life out of me. I thought you'd fallen into the water."

He reached out a muddy finger and gently wiped a tear from my cheek. "Don't cry, Hannah. Pa don't allow me by the creek unless someone's with me."

I wrapped my arms around him and felt his soft, red hair against my face. A little more mud didn't matter. We walked together up the road toward home with Ruff bounding after us.

Chapter 4

Pa stood at the bottom of the stairs calling. I raised my head, and through the small window, saw the sky, slate blue and sprinkled with stars. Dawn was still a ways off. I burrowed my head in the pillow, not wanting to leave the warmth of my bed. Then, remembering it was Sunday, I eased out onto the cold floor. Chores and milking had to be done early so we could make the two hour drive to Brockton and be on time for church at 10:00. Must be right annoying to Bess and Molly, being expected to give milk in the middle of the night.

I shook Nellie, who moaned but slid out of bed. With teeth chattering, we buttoned into our Sunday best and climbed down the stairs toward the welcome warmth radiating from the wood stove. Of late, the days had been pleasant, but the nights were still cold.

By the time Pa and Caleb came in from the barn, Willy was up and dressed, and griddle cakes were ready. I was right proud of my success with griddle cakes. Even Caleb grudgingly agreed to have seconds.

"Wouldn't be right to waste food when some folks go hungry," he said.

I couldn't see as how his eating a second helping would do those hungry folks any good, but I kept quiet as he stacked his plate and poured on molasses syrup.

As we drove out to the dirt road, the sky was the soft pussy willow-gray that precedes dawn. A scattering of birds chirped in the cool, damp air. Nellie and I sat in the back of the wagon huddled under a quilt with Willy between us, while Caleb sat up front with Pa.

"Doesn't seem right that we should leave the farm unattended, what with that mountain cat prowling about," said Caleb, tugging at the collar of his Sunday shirt.

He must have figured Pa would be of a mind to leave him home to look after the place, but he should know him better than that.

Pa pulled on the reins, turning Dolly and Dan onto the main track. "We do all we can to take care of things. Then we have to trust the Lord. We can't stay home every Sunday to guard the sheep. Haven't seen any lion tracks around. It's possible he's left the area. Ruff can keep watch while we're gone."

Willy was quick to agree. "Yeah. That old cat come around, Ruff'd chase him clean out of the valley."

They had more faith in Ruff than I did. He'd high-tail it under the porch at the first sign of danger. I kept my thoughts to myself, for I didn't wish to be reminded that it was my fault the cougar was still prowling about.

We rolled down the rutted road, bouncing over bumps and splashing through puddles of muddy water. There had been a light rain yesterday, but Pa reckoned the roads would be dry enough for travel. Despite the jostling, I was near to dozing off, until with a sudden jolt, the wagon stopped. The team strained at the traces, but we weren't moving.

"Easy, Dan. Whoa, Dolly." Pa turned to us. "Horses are going to need our help." You'd expect he might have used stronger words, but that wasn't Pa's way. The right front wheel was mired hub deep in a hole filled with muddy water.

"We'll be needing a log to lever the wheel up. Caleb, you come with me. Rest of you get some rocks and dirt ready for filling the hole. There's a shovel under the seat." Pa grabbed his ax and headed toward the creek bottom where cottonwoods lined the bank. He didn't seem to consider we were wearing our

Sunday clothes. It was certain Ma would have.

Willy found an old pail in the wagon and ran about gathering rocks. Nellie and I took turns shoveling loose dirt into a pile next to the mired wheel. Finally, with a sigh, Nellie dropped the shovel, "I'm thinking that ought to be enough dirt to fill two holes. Let's sit on this rock and wait for Pa and Caleb." She brushed the surface and sat down. I had to smile. There was more dirt on her face than there was on the rock.

Slanting rays of morning sun cast a golden glow across the desert, intensifying the green of early spring cottonwoods and sage. Brilliant pink blossoms were opening on clumps of cactus plants, and desert primrose dotted the ground with white. To the north, red rock cliffs rose in front of blue mountains topped with snow. I took a deep breath of the cool air, fragrant with sage and wild flowers. A feeling of peace swept over me.

The tranquillity was interrupted when Willie called, "Hannah, see what I found!" He ran toward me swinging his bucket, side-stepping rocks and cactus plants. I didn't want to look. I hoped it wasn't a snake.

He held out the pail. "Look! Lizards. They're my new pets, Sam and Ezra."

"Willy, you can't keep them. They'll die. Best let them go."

"Will not die," he insisted. "I'll catch flies and stuff for them to eat. I can build a nice house for them. They'll like it."

I was sure they wouldn't like it, but I had a hard time telling Willy no. All he had to do was look at me with those blue eyes—eyes like Ma's.

"Well, put some dirt and a little water in the bucket. And put something on top so's they can't climb out. Don't want them crawling around in the wagon."

Nellie looked at me and shook her head in disbelief. "You going to let him keep those creatures? You'll doubtless be sorry you gave in to his sweet-talk."

Just about that time, Pa and Caleb came into view lugging a log up from the creek. When they reached the road, they carried it to the wagon and positioned it under the front axle. Pa rolled a rock over, and levered the wagon up, giving us room to push the dirt and rocks under the wheel. Pa climbed in and urged the horses forward. With a lurch, the wagon rolled out of the hole. Then after looking us over, Pa ordered us down to the creek to wash off the worst of the red dirt.

I could hear the water before I saw it. The stream had subsided some, but still appeared to be a churning menace. I couldn't bear to go near the bank. I gripped Willy's arm before he could run to the edge.

"Never saw such a scaredy-cat," taunted Caleb. "You try'n to make a sissy out of Willy, too?"

Pa gave him a stern look, then soaked his handkerchief in the cold, silty water, and we washed. When Pa decided we were as clean as we were going to get, we returned to the wagon and continued on down the road. It was fortunate we'd started early. Any more mud holes and we'd be lucky to be in Brockton by noon.

As we rumbled along, the morning sun rested on the rock cliffs where green sage and junipers clung stubbornly in every crevasse and crack of the red canyon walls. I grudgingly admitted to myself that it was beautiful, but so lonely. Not a living soul in any direction.

Then suddenly, I caught sight of movement on the eastern horizon. Silhouetted against the light, three mounted riders came over the ridge. My heart thudded against my ribs. The braids, their dress—they were Indians. *Black Hawk!* Word of his renegade band had spread throughout the territory. Were these his men—or Chief Charumpeak's Paiutes who traded with us? I tugged on Pa's shirt and pointed toward the ridge.

He turned and watched as the braves made their way down

the slope towards us. Caleb reached under the wagon seat for the rifle, but Pa shook his head. "No, leave the gun there. We won't be needing it."

"But Pa, all the talk of Indian trouble," I said.

He didn't answer, just climbed slowly out of the wagon and walked back to meet them. I sat frozen, hardly daring to breathe while Pa and the braves exchanged signs and grunted words. When the Indians turned and rode back toward the ridge, I let my breath out. Pa stood watching, then raised his hand in a sign they returned. It took a good long while for my heart to stop pounding. I'd never feared Indians before, but with all the talk of trouble and being so far from the safety of home, every brave looked to be one of Black Hawk's band.

"No cause to worry." Pa climbed into the wagon. "That was a Paiute hunting party." He took the reins from Caleb, and we rolled on down the road.

"Hope they don't decide our sheep would make for good hunting, seeing as we're not there to protect them," said Caleb.

"Chuarumpeak and his son Saugawa were here when we came to the valley six years ago. I started trading with their people as soon as I had something to trade. It was hard those first years. They showed us how to make flour from mesquite beans. Their squaws brought us pine nuts and ope berries. Saugawa's as honest as any man in the territory. I consider him a friend. As long as we deal fairly with them, we'll have no trouble from the Paiutes."

"Doesn't seem like even trading," Caleb said. "A few pine nuts, baskets, or pots in exchange for corn, molasses, and the like."

Pa stared straight ahead. "You haven't seen how the Indians in this part of the country struggle to survive. Our settlements have taken land where they hunted—made it hard for them to feed their people. They're too proud to beg, so we trade. I don't worry when the trading isn't even. When settlers ignore Brother Brigham's admonition to feed the Indians rather than fight them, trouble follows. We can't expect the Lord's blessings if we fail to help the poor."

Pa'd be reading to us from Matthew again. " . . . *inasmuch as ye have done it unto one of the least of these my brethren. . . .*"

Pa was right. The Paiutes had never caused us any trouble, but with all the stories of Black Hawk, I hoped we wouldn't meet any more Indians today.

Chapter 5

Strains of music drifted towards us as our wagon rolled into Brockton. Pa pulled out his pocket watch and confirmed that we were fifteen minutes late for the ten o'clock meeting. That was no surprise. Considering the interruptions, the horses had done right well. We pulled into a field where other wagons were parked, and Pa hurried us towards the red stone church.

The door squeaked as we entered, but singing masked the sound. Pa put his finger to his lips, and we tiptoed to the back bench, Caleb first, followed by Pa, Nellie, Willy, and me. The inside of the church seemed dim and cool after a morning in the bright sun. Three tall windows on each side of the chapel provided light, and through those on the east, rectangles of sunlight slanted across the room. A faint smell of wool and mothballs came from Sunday clothes brought out of trunks for the Sabbath.

We opened our hymn books to join the singing, but before I found the page, the hymn ended. The hard wooden benches creaked as the congregation sat down. "How much longer, Hannah?" Willy asked as the speaker headed to the pulpit. His voice carried across the quiet room, and faces turned toward us. Most folks smiled, but Pa scowled, his stern look directed at me. I hushed Willy and decided being late was a blessing. He squirmed about, then stuck his hand in his jacket pocket and settled back on the bench. Must have brought his collection of rocks. I prayed they wouldn't clatter onto the floor, but for the moment he was quiet.

I turned my attention to the speaker who was talking about Job and his patience and gratitude. Pa sure didn't need a sermon on gratitude. I'd heard enough from him on *that* subject. I looked toward the front of the chapel where Eliza, Henry, and Charles sat with their family. I was right taken by the way Charles' dark hair curled above his collar. I felt my face flush. Not more than two years ago he had been as bothersome as a wasp at a picnic, always teasing Eliza and me, chasing us with snakes and such. Now I was beguiled by his brown eyes, his crooked grin, and the dimple in his chin. He'd passed me up in height, and when I stood next to him, I felt almost dainty. Best thing though, he'd begun to treat me like a friend. I hoped we'd be eating our lunch with the Whitlocks as we usually did between meetings. My mind drifted into a dream where Charles and I waltzed across the Social Hall floor--then Willy scrambled off the bench.

"Hannah, catch Ezra," he said in a loud whisper. I looked down to see two brown lizards scuttling under the bench in front of me. Willy, flat on his stomach, scooted after them. I grabbed his legs and pulled.

"Stop it, Hannah. Ezra's getting away!" he yelled, all attempts at whispering forgotten. There was a gasp from Sister Mattson two rows in front of us. Doubtless, she had become acquainted with Ezra. Squeals and suppressed giggles echoed through the chapel. Bishop Crawford stopped his sermon in mid-sentence. Pa rose, scooped up a struggling Willy, grabbed me by the arm, and strode out the door as the congregation turned and stared. How could Pa humiliate me this way when the disturbance was Willy's doing? I was just grateful we were sitting on the back row.

Once outside, Pa put Willy down and faced us. "Have I not taught my children respect for the Lord's house?" he asked. His brown eyes bore into us under thick brows, his face red with anger.

"Pa, I didn't know he had the lizards in his pocket. I thought

26

they were in the wagon."

"*Lizards?*" he thundered. "You brought lizards into the church?"

Willy's mind was not on the desecration of a sacred place. "Hannah made me lose Ezra," he pouted. "I could've caught him 'cept she grabbed hold of my legs. Now I only got Sam, and his tail came off." He looked at me accusingly.

"He'll likely grow a new one." Pa led Willy to the edge of the churchyard. "Turn it loose," he ordered. Scowling, Willy did as he was told. Pa turned toward the church. "We'd best get back to the meeting. Perhaps you'll learn to behave more reverently."

I didn't want to go in and face all those people, but I knew better than to argue with Pa now. It was plain he'd not yet adopted the patience of Job. I came close to smiling at the thought, but deemed it unwise. As we filed back to our seats, Caleb aimed a smirk in my direction. I didn't understand what had made him so cantankerous of late. Nellie looked at me and shrugged her shoulders. Then I recalled her words: "You going to let him keep those creatures? You'll doubtless be sorry you gave in to his sweet-talk." I should have listened.

After the meeting, as folks visited in front of the church, Pa made his way over to Matthew Crawford. "Bishop," he said, "I'm sorry my family caused such a ruckus in the middle of your sermon."

"Don't worry one bit about it, Isaac. Why, I do believe half the congregation was asleep at the time. Sure brought 'em to attention. I don't think a soul dozed off after that. I'm just glad you were able to get here, what with the roads being flooded and all."

"We hit one bad spot that mired the front wheel. Slowed us down a bit, but the roads were passable other than that," said Pa.

"How are you folks faring up there? I know it's not been easy without Caroline. Anything we can do, let us know."

Bishop Crawford's a fine man. I truly appreciated what he said, but I was not so fond of Maude Winkle. She was waddling our way, waving her white gloved hand. I had a mind to leave, but Pa held my arm.

"Brother York," she gushed, "it's so good to see you and your lovely children out to meeting this beautiful morning. And just look at you, Hannah. What a fine big girl. My how you've grown. You must be most as tall as your Pa!"

"Yes, ma'am." I saw the grin on Caleb's face and knew I'd not heard the end of that remark.

"Nice to see you, Sister Winkle," said Pa. Then he turned to me. "We'll be eating our lunch at the Whitlock's place. Eliza's wanting you to walk with her. I expect you to help Sister Whitlock with lunch, so you'd best hurry. Willy can ride with me."

Pa knew I'd been yearning to talk to Eliza. Must be, he was repenting for the way he'd shamed me in front of the whole congregation. I felt an urge to throw my arms around his neck, but I held back, and the moment passed.

"Thank you, Pa," was all I said. Then I ran off to find Eliza.

Chapter 6

A breeze scented with apple blossoms blew across the shaded porch where Pa and Brother Whitlock were discussing crops, religion, and politics. Eliza and I brought out ham, cheese, and a plate of Sister Whitlock's fresh homemade bread while Nellie poured cold milk from a pewter pitcher. Then the three of us spread an old quilt under the apple tree where white blossoms fluttered down like snow. I'd heard all I cared to about sheep, pigs, and the sugar cane crop. I wanted news of goings on in Brockton.

"Guess you heard Miss Gooding up and married some fellow name of Wilcox," reported Eliza. "Went off to California with him. I heard some women in town say she'd live to regret it, but the girls at school thought it best, she being close to twenty-eight and near a spinster." She went on to describe in glowing terms, a shipment of piece good that had arrived at the mercantile. Then right in the middle of a report on budding romances, Brother Whitlock's words caught my attention.

"—mountain cat was likely a young male out looking for new territory. They're not good hunters like the older cats. Most likely your sheep looked like easy prey."

"Haven't seen any sign of him of late," said Pa. "The shot must have scared him off, but I reckon it's possible he'll come back." Caleb attempted to tell his side of the story, but Pa stopped him.

By now the men had our attention, and we listened to Brother Whitlock.

"There's plenty to worry about without having to fret about cougars, off by ourselves as we are. Bishop Crawford's concerned about the safety of his sister Annie. She and the children are traveling from Manti with her husband and his brother."

"From what I hear, they plan on settling in Brockton," said Pa.

"Yes. James is a skilled stone mason. He and his brother Orson hope to get a business going. Annie's to teach school come fall. Since Mary Gooding left, we're sorely in need of a teacher."

"When are they expected?" asked Pa.

"Bishop thought they'd arrive before now."

Pa leaned back in his chair. "Weather's not been good for traveling."

"That's true. Still, with Black Hawk's men riled up like they are, rustling and raiding, it's a real worry. Some farmers have lost most of their livestock. Now we hear they've killed a family over by Pipe Springs." A shiver ran through me as I remembered the Indians on the butte, silhouetted against the morning sun.

The two hours between meetings passed quickly. After tidying up, we rode the short distance back to the church and found seats next to the Whitlocks. Pa made sure he sat by Willy. Seemed a bit late for that, since the lizards were gone. I was happy though, to sit by Eliza and Charles. As folks entered and found seats, some directed smiles in our direction. Guess they hadn't forgotten the entertainment we'd provided earlier.

At two o'clock with the chapel close to full, the meeting began with a song and prayer. Then as Bishop Crawford walked to the pulpit, the door burst open and a stranger hurried up the aisle, spurs rattling as he strode past us. His chaps and shirt were covered with red dirt, and he held a battered hat in his hand. Sweat from the band had run down his face leaving trails in the dust. It was plain he'd been riding hard and hadn't come for the meeting. A low murmur arose from the congregation. As he spoke to Bishop Crawford, the color drained from his face. He left the pulpit and followed the stranger up the aisle and out the door.

"Pa, what's happening?" I asked.

He put a hand on my shoulder and said, "I'm not sure. You watch the others. I may be needed." He stood, and left the building with Brother Whitlock and Brother Clement.

The murmuring continued as the congregation waited for someone to take charge. Minutes passed before Brother Clement returned and walked to the front of the chapel. He stood for a moment, then cleared his throat and spoke, his voice somber. "Bishop Crawford received word that his brother-in-law and others traveling in his party have been killed by Indians. He's asked me to dismiss the meeting."

My heart froze. Did that mean Annie was dead? At first, everyone sat there stunned, unable to move. Then they stood and filed out of the chapel talking in hushed voices. Women, wiping away tears, wept silently. Sister Whitlock turned to us. "You children wait here. I'm going to see if I can be of help." She put an arm around Sister Crawford, and they hurried out together.

I felt numb and sick. I'd met Annie Thornton, her husband, James, and their children last summer. What reason did the Indians have for killing them?

A tear rolled down Nellie's cheek. "How will we get home?" she asked.

"Same way we got here. Pa's not afraid of no Indians," said Caleb. He tried to sound brave, but a tremor in his voice revealed fear. Still, he had no cause to snap at Nellie that way.

I put my arm around her. "It's going to be all right." What else could I say?

As the minutes ticked by, I began to fidget. I never have been much for just sitting and waiting. When close to an hour had passed and Pa wasn't back, I decided to do something about it. "Can't bear to sit here any longer," I said. "I'm going looking for Pa."

"You best not," said Charles. "Can't tell what you might find out there."

"Don't reckon I'll run into Black Hawk."

"Don't reckon so. Could be something near as bad though. I'll come along. Caleb can stay with the others."

Caleb nodded. Not a word of back-talk. I followed Charles out into the bright afternoon sun. "Good thing it wasn't me telling him what to do," I said.

"He just doesn't take well to orders coming from a girl, that's all," Charles replied.

Seemed it must be more than that, but I didn't say so.

The dirt road in front of the church was deserted. It looked as though all life had disappeared from Brockton. Charles led the way down the empty street past adobe and log houses to the center of town. Wasn't much there, just the mercantile, post office, and Doctor Hulett's home and office on the right, and on the left, the social hall, barbershop, the blacksmith forge, and a few more houses. A scrawny cat ran across the road. A little girl peered at us from behind a curtained window. Some distance away, a dog howled. And though the sun was hot, a shiver ran through me.

We followed the road as it curved toward the livery stable with its smell of horses and leather. From there, it wasn't but a short distance to Bishop Crawford's farm where I was sure we'd find Pa. Then suddenly Charles stopped. "Listen," he said. A murmur of voices came from behind the stable. I was certain one of them belonged to Pa.

Charles put a hand on my shoulder. "Might be best you

don't go back there." I paid him no mind. He followed as I walked around the side of the stable, sidestepping piles of manure. At the corner of the building, I stopped and leaned against the rough gray boards. My legs could scarce hold me, and I grabbed Charles' arm.

"Shouldn't have come," he said, his voice a hoarse whisper.

Three bodies lay on a piece of canvas spread out on the ground, one just a boy. Dark patches of dried blood crusted their clothes and their matted hair. Three empty coffins waited near by. I covered my mouth and stepped back around the corner--away from the horror.

We heard Dr. Hulett's voice. "Best not to delay the burial, being as how they've been out there close to two days."

"Men are digging the graves now." It was Pa's voice. "Should be ready within the hour."

"Good. How's Annie holding up?"

I didn't want to hear more. "Let's go," I whispered. I didn't want Pa to see us. I was grateful Annie was alive, but my heart ached for her sorrow.

We walked back to the church, neither of us saying much. Sister Whitlock had sent word that we were to wait there for her. When Nellie asked where we'd been, I told her I was in town looking for Pa. Couldn't bring myself to say more. I didn't want to think of what I'd seen behind the livery stable.

Soon Sister Whitlock arrived in their wagon to take us to the burial. We rode to a hill behind the town where church members had gathered. Three mounds of dirt marked the open graves. Pa stood with Bishop Crawford and Brother Clement, while Sister Crawford wrapped a comforting arm around Annie Thornton. Her daughter Sarah, a little girl with blond curls, nestled against her side. One of the graves had been dug for David, her twelve-year-old son.

My mind wandered back to two other graves on a hillside at

home. I remembered standing there on that cloudy October day, full of grief, but with no tears left to shed. They had soaked my pillow and seeped into the ground near the lilac bush where I had lain, grieving over Ma and Jenny.

Bishop Crawford spoke of the lives of James Thornton, his brother Orson, and the boy, David. Pa prayed and the service was over. Annie Thornton looked pale and worn as she took her daughter's hand and walked down the hill with her brother.

It was near six o'clock by the time we climbed in our wagon for the trip home. We'd likely need the lantern before we drove onto our lane. Pa assured us that there was no danger traveling on this road away from Brockton. I hoped he was right. I couldn't rightly believe that it was still Sunday. Seemed like days ago that we had left the farm. We rode in silence for a time, everyone thinking his own thoughts. Willy put his head in my lap and was soon asleep.

Finally Nellie spoke. "Pa, how did Annie and Sarah get away from the Indians?"

Pa didn't answer for a spell. Then he told us what had happened.

"They'd left Manti early in the morning. Some folks had warned them to wait until they could travel with another wagon, but they were anxious to leave and didn't put much stock in the rumors about Indian trouble in the area. Late in the afternoon, they saw a band of Indians riding toward them waving rifles, whooping and hollering. James pulled up behind a clump of trees and sent Annie and the children to hide in the brush. When the Indians started shooting, David jumped up and ran to his father. They killed him."

Pa cleared his throat, then continued. "Annie and Sarah stayed hidden until the Indians rode off. When she went back to the wagon, the three were dead and the horses gone. Annie covered the bodies, and they waited by the trees until a wagon and riders came along and brought them to Brockton."

We rode along in the fading light, Nellie with her head on my shoulder. I wanted to erase the terrifying images from my mind, but I couldn't. I'd seen and heard too much today. Now every movement—wind bending the sage or a bird shaking a branch set my heart to racing. At each turn, I feared that a band of warriors would appear on a ridge and swoop down on us. When we finally reached the farm, I was limp and exhausted.

Why had Pa brought us here? No doctor for miles. A stream that floods its banks and washes away crops, or dries up and leaves them wilting in the blazing heat. Painted savages killing innocent people. The Indians could have their wretched land back for all I cared.

Chapter 7

The days following our trip to Brockton, I could scarce keep my mind off the things I'd seen—three bodies laid out on the ground. It seemed like the grief of Ma's passing was thrust back on me, and the hurt was raw again. I wondered, would Bishop Crawford be telling Annie Thornton that the Lord never gives us more than we can bear? Would she believe it?

Thursday morning after breakfast, Pa sent Nellie and me out to plant beans, squash, and potatoes. As we set to work, the sun crept over the red cliffs sending our long shadows over the tilled ground. Bees buzzed around the lilacs, while meadowlarks filled the air with song. Nellie stopped at the end of a row and leaned on her hoe. "It's right pleasant working outside."

I bent down and picked up a handful of damp soil and let it sift through my fingers. "Ma always said there wasn't anything like working in God's good earth to cheer a body up." Fact was, the morning sun and gentle breeze seemed to be pushing the gloom right out of my heart.

Pa and the boys were in a nearby field planting a second crop of corn and a large watermelon patch. Pa traded the produce he raised for wheat and such. Folks said his orchard and garden produced the finest fruit around.

Late in the morning, Caleb walked toward the vegetable patch and called, "Us men are wanting our dinner."

"Men?" I asked.

Caleb scowled. "Been doing a man's work, and it's well past meal-time."

It wasn't meal-time, and did he think Nellie and I had been

standing around all morning smelling the lilacs? I didn't ask, didn't want to rile him more. "We'll bring it out when it's ready," I said. He spun around and stalked off across the field.

As I watched him go, a sadness swept over me, for I remembered when he had been my best friend. He was six and I was eight when we moved from Salt Lake to the southern part of the Utah Territory. Must have been hard on Ma, just settling into one home, then picking up and moving again. We had arrived in December, and that winter, the rain came down in torrents . We lived in our wagon box and a tent, neither one able to keep out all the rain. Don't rightly know how Ma managed, but I don't recall her ever complaining. To Caleb and me, it had seemed like an adventure.

In the spring, Ma had worked alongside Pa making adobe bricks for the walls of our new house. Caleb and I had delighted in mixing the mud and straw, then turning the bricks as they dried and hardened under the hot sun. Nellie, just five, wouldn't be left out. Ma would look at us, smile, and shake her head. "My land," she'd say, "there looks to be more mud on you children than there is in the bricks. I do hope there'll be enough left to finish the house."

The years that followed, Caleb and I worked and played together. Now he balked at my every request and could scarcely wait to point out my mistakes. Seems when Ma died, the laughter died with her—and I'd lost Caleb as a friend.

Nellie and I went in, fixed dinner, and carried it out to the melon patch where raucous cries filled the air. Gulls circled above the furrows, then glided to a landing on the fresh-turned earth to snatch up fat worms uncovered by the plow. I couldn't believe all that squabbling over a bunch of slimy worms.

Nellie had declared that on such a fine day it seemed only right that we have a picnic. We set food out on a quilt in the shade of a cottonwood. Pa and the boys joined us with Ruff bounding after them.

"Keep that mangy brown dog off the blanket," I ordered.

"Ruff is not mangy." Willy wrapped an arm around his neck. "Are you, boy?"

"And he sure ain't brown." said Caleb. "You and him both got hair the exact color as them red rocks yonder." I ignored his insult, remembering that Ma always said my hair was auburn, not red. And I never did hear of an auburn dog.

We ate corn cake with cheese, and apples from the root cellar, washing it all down with milk cooled in the spring. Willy watched the gulls as he gulped down his food. Then he ran off after them followed by Ruff, who was always ready for a chase. The gulls scolded, and with shrill cries, took to the air.

Nellie laughed and shook her head. "Willy sure enough wants to catch himself a pet."

"We can be grateful the birds are fast," said Pa with a smile. Then he turned to me. "Caleb says you're near finished in the vegetable patch."

"Just a row of potatoes left. Nellie and I were thinking we ought to plant some flowers around the house when we're finished with the vegetables."

"Plant them if you must," he said and walked back to the plow.

I sat there puzzled by Pa's attitude. "What should we do?" I asked.

"Best we plant the flowers," said Nellie. "Ma'd be right disappointed if we don't." Nellie always acted like Ma was hovering about, making sure we carried on as she would have done.

"You're right. We'll plant them. I couldn't stand the look of the place without some daisies around." Nellie and I picked up the picnic supplies and walked back to the house.

We finished planting the potatoes and the flower seeds Ma

had saved: poppies, daisies, marigold, asters, and blue bells. Then Nellie gathered eggs while I weeded around the violets. While I knelt there, surrounded by their fragrance, I heard hoof-beats on the road. Wasn't often that anyone came by this way. I jumped up, my heart pounding. So much had changed. No more than a week ago, I would have welcomed the arrival of visitors. I looked toward the road, and fear vanished as Charles Whitlock turned off the track onto our lane. Truth is though, my heart kept right on thumping as he got off his horse and walked toward me.

"Stage came in with a letter for your father. Pa thought it best that I bring it over. Said it might be important. And I've been wanting to know how you were doing. What you saw— wasn't a thing a girl should see."

"Shouldn't anyone have to," I said. Then we stood there, neither of us knowing what to say next. Finally I found my voice. "Pa will be grateful you brought the mail. It's near time for supper. You're welcome to stay."

"Thanks, but I have to hurry back. Guess you'll be coming for church on Sunday." He grinned, and a most enjoyable feeling swept over me.

I nodded and smiled. "Pa will see to it that we do." I gazed after him as he walked back to his horse. "Wait," I called. I left him standing there while I ran into the house and wrapped a napkin around an apple dumpling, then raced back out and handed it to him. "I baked dumplings yesterday. You can eat one on the way."

Charles smiled. "Thanks," he said. He put his foot in the stirrup and swung onto the pinto's back. "Well, I'll see you come Sunday."

"Thanks for riding over," I called as he trotted onto the main track. I stood there for a time, staring down the road, giddy at the thought of seeing him again.

So distracted was I by Charles' smile that I almost forgot the letter. I regained my senses and looked at the envelope. Judging from the wrinkles and smudges, it had traveled a considerable distance, but the penmanship was beautiful. I glanced at the return address.

Miss Margaret Ann Dalton
416 Dearington Place
Boston, Massachusetts

Ma's older sister. I had never seen her, but knew that she taught school in Boston. Ma had corresponded with her for a time, but it had been more than two years since she had written. It was doubtless a letter of sympathy, but what else would she write to make the envelope bulge so? I hoped Pa would hurry home, for I hate to be left in suspense. I was most curious to know what Aunt Margaret had to say.

Chapter 8

I slipped the letter into my apron pocket and went in to start supper. With a fire in the wood stove and the afternoon sun shining through the west windows, the room grew uncomfortably warm. I left the doors open, hoping the breeze would cool the room and banish the smell of frying chops without attracting a swarm of flies. The aroma of lilacs wafted in and mingled with the smell of corn cake and mutton. The meat sizzled in the fry pan. Outside, magpies squabbled over scraps of seed potato left from planting. When the buzzing flies drowned out the birds, Nellie grabbed the swatter and started swinging. I figured we'd best shut the door.

Ruff barked, the gate creaked, and I knew Pa and the boys were headed for the house. I opened the door and called, "Make sure you clean your shoes," then slammed it shut before Caleb could complain about my bossiness. He must have been fuming as they stomped and scraped, but all the scraping in the world couldn't get rid of the smell of cows and manure. While Pa put the pails of milk in the lean-to, I set the food on the table.

Caleb wrinkled his nose. "Smells like mutton again."

"Sheep, pigs, and chickens—that's what we raise, so that's what we eat," said Pa.

"Be grateful for the bounties we're blessed with. Many are not so fortunate." With that reminder, we knelt for the blessing.

Once the food was blessed and passed, I took the letter out of my pocket and handed it to Pa. "Charles brought it over. Said it came this morning on the stage." Pa studied the envelope and laid it aside without a word. I reckon he didn't want to read it before we ate, since there's nothing worse than cold mutton when the grease sets.

When supper was cleared away and dishes done, Pa sat at the table and stared at the envelope in his hand. I felt the urge to grab it and rip it open myself, but of course I didn't. "Well, Pa, aren't you going to read it?" I asked. Nellie and I hovered over him, and Caleb didn't hide his interest, for not much mail came our way.

"It's from Boston, from your Ma's sister Margaret." He opened the envelope, took the letter out, and started to read:

> *My dear brother-in-law Isaac,*
>
> *It was with deep sorrow that I received word of the death of my sister Caroline. I regret that the distance between us was such that I was unable to see her, and now, never will again. I want to express my deepest sympathy to you and the children. I'm sure it's been difficult for them without their mother.*
>
> *This brings me to my second reason for writing. I have obtained leave from my teaching position and have arranged for passage on the stage bound for Utah. I will be leaving in four weeks. I trust that I will be of comfort and help. The welfare of the children is of utmost concern to me.*
>
> *Because of this concern, I am enclosing detailed information about the girl's school where I teach. If it meets with your approval, I would like to bring the girls east and enroll them here. Our standards are high, providing our pupils with the best possible education.*
>
> *I'm sure Caroline would want this for them. We can discuss the matter when I arrive.*

Along with the school brochure, I am enclosing a letter from my parents. I'm sure they regret their misunderstandings with Caroline.

Respectfully,
Your sister-in-law, Margaret

"Your aunt's a woman of action and always speaks her mind," Pa said.

"I think we can expect her to arrive sometime next month." His face showed no sign of emotion, and his words left me to wonder what he was thinking.

Then he read the short letter from Grandpa and Grandma Dalton. I had never seen them—only pictures where they looked strict and unfriendly. Ma had assured me that the stern expressions were the result of sitting motionless for the photographer and not an indication of sour dispositions.

Pa sat for a time in silence. It tries my patience when he does this, but Pa ponders his words before he speaks. I'm sure he wishes I would adopt the practice. "Your Ma's parents never could forgive her for joining the church and marrying me," he said at last. "Must have been hard for them to write. I don't imagine they quite knew what to say. Still, it was good that they sent their regards to you children."

That night as I lay in bed, a flurry of thoughts swirled through my head like leaves tossed by the wind. Boston, a city with neighbors no more than a short skip away. No wild animals. No Indians to worry about. A real school with hundreds of books. No raging rivers. But Charles—there would be no Charles in Boston. And no Eliza. I'd miss them dearly. And who did Aunt Margaret think would look after Willy? At this thought, I must have sighed, for Nellie poked me.

"You think Pa's going to send us to Boston with Aunt

Margaret?" she asked.

"I don't hardly think so. Who'd do the cooking?" We giggled at the thought of Caleb stirring up a batch of biscuits.

"Know what I'm thinking?" she asked. "Aunt Margaret's getting on in years. Way I figure, she must be at least thirty-eight. I'm thinking she might just have a mind to come out here and get herself a husband."

"Where's she going to find a man in this wilderness?"

"Well, Pa, of course! In the letter she called him, 'My dear Isaac.' Bet she plans on taking us all back to Boston."

"Land sakes, Nellie, she'd not get Pa away from the farm unless she tied him up and dragged him. And it doesn't appear to me that Aunt Margaret would take to farm life."

"Good. I don't fancy the idea of her taking Ma's place."

I patted her shoulder. "No need to worry about that tonight. Stage most likely won't get here for a month or more. Let's go to sleep."

That night my dreams took me to Boston. I was wearing a dress and bonnet of sage green satin that looked right nice with my rock red hair. I was walking down a shady boardwalk with Charles. Funny though, he was dressed in homespuns and work boots. Then, just as he was about to whisper something in my ear, Willy stumbled out of bed looking for the chamber pot.

I was most anxious to hear what Charles had to say, but a dream's not like a book. I couldn't put it down and get back to it later. After Willy climbed back in bed, I walked to the window and looked out toward the line of cottonwoods. Moonlight flooded the yard. Gaps between the tree trunks revealed the creek, a gleaming silver serpent, quietly slipping through the trees. Weeks of dry weather had tamed it.

As I stood there thinking it was a right pretty sight, Ruff gave a short bark and trotted out through the gate. Then I saw Pa walking toward the house. He slapped his leg and Ruff ran to him, wagging joyfully. Pa bent down and scratched his head. Then giving him a pat, they came through the gate together. It must have been well past midnight. What did Pa do out there while the rest of us slept? The door creaked and the bolt eased into place. No candlelight flickered from below. And just as before, on that stormy night, Pa moved quietly across the kitchen to his room.

Chapter 9

At the end of April with the crops in, Pa turned his attention to the sheep. After breakfast, he and the boys headed out to the paddock where the woolly critters waited for their yearly clipping. Charles and his father were riding over to help. Ordinarily I'm not fond of shearing day, but this year I was right happy Nellie and I were asked to wash the fleece. I'd baked corn bread and molasses cookies the day before, and ham hock and beans simmered outside in the brick oven. Just before we joined the men in the sheep yard, I put my hair in a braid and tied it with a light green ribbon. Nellie looked at me and frowned. "Those sheep don't care what you look like. Must be Charles you're gussied up for." She smiled a knowing smile. Had it been anyone but Nellie taking notice of my vanity, I'd have been mortified. Charles wouldn't expect me to be washing fleece in my Sunday best—still, the green ribbon couldn't hurt.

As we neared the shearing shed, we were met by the sound of bleating sheep and a "Morning, Hannah. Morning, Nellie," from Charles. His brown eyes crinkled at the corners when he smiled. I was right glad I'd thought to wear that ribbon.

Steam from the scouring vat rose in the cool morning air, carrying with it the smell of homemade lye soap. Next to this vat where Nellie and I would wash the fleece was the rinsing trough. Pa had diverted water from the spring so that it flowed into the trough and out again. That way there would always be clean rinse water. Pa was right clever when it came to mechanical things.

Soon the sheep yard was a bustle of activity. Ruff nudged the sheep and herded them through the gate of the holding pen where they were grabbed and carried to the shearing platform. The men clipped the wool so that it rolled off in one piece. It's a mystery to me how they do it. Caleb was there to learn, and also to lead the naked sheep out into the paddock. The poor things looked mighty peculiar with their wool gone. When bundles of fleece were brought to the scouring vat, we dropped them into the soapy bath. As the steam rose, Nellie scrunched up her nose. "Can't say I'm fond of the smell of lye soap and wet wool."

We gripped our paddles and sloshed the fleece about in the sudsy water. When dirt and grass settled to the bottom, we lifted the wool with our paddles and dumped it with a splash into the rinse trough. From there it went to the drying racks. The wet fleece was surprisingly heavy. My arms ached, rivers of sweat ran down my face, and damp strands of hair escaped from my braid and hung limply around my face. I was too busy to worry about it. It was all we could do to keep up with the shearing.

The morning became a blur of bleating sheep, sloshing paddles, and the smell of wet wool that grew stronger as fleece piled up on the racks. I shuddered when I thought of what would follow—hours of carding, dyeing, spinning, weaving, and knitting. And the soap! We'd soon be needing to make more soap from lard and cottonwood ashes. It made me tired just to think about it, and I was already tuckered out.

Pa came over about mid-day and said they were nearly done shearing. They'd finish up the scouring so we could get the dinner set out. Nellie, glad to be through with the job, dashed off toward the house. As I walked past the sheep pen, Charles came around the corner, stopped and smiled. "That's a mighty pretty ribbon," he said. "Looks right fine with the red in your hair."

I didn't know what to say, and to hear Caleb tell it, I'm

never speechless, but I wasn't used to compliments. Finally I managed to mumble, "I'm partial to green myself." As he smiled and walked away, I turned and called, "Won't be long till dinner!"

Suddenly the aches were gone. I fairly skipped to the house. If I hurried, I'd have time to change my dress. "What in tarnation is the matter with you, Hannah York?" I asked myself. "You're acting like a ninny." I just hoped Charles liked molasses cookies!

Chapter 10

Two days after the shearing, Nellie and I sat upstairs in the spinning room surrounded by bundles of matted fleece and stacks of carded wool. It was quiet in the house, what with Pa and the boys down in the pasture. The only sounds came from Ma's clock ticking in the corner of the room and the steady rasping of our carding blocks, rectangles of wood covered with fine wire teeth. We combed the tangled wads of fleece between the blocks, transforming them into soft fluffs of wool. Everything in this room reminded me of Ma—the clock, the spinning wheel, the loom, and the rag rugs that covered the floor.

I placed a fluff of wool on the pile. "Remember how Ma used to sit here tearing old clothes into strips? She'd laugh and say she'd made so many rag rugs and quilts, she sometimes wished the rag man would come and haul all the old clothes away."

Nellie nodded. "I love those quilts. When I wrap one around me, feels like Ma's with me."

The time passed quietly, just Nellie and me with our thoughts, the carding blocks rasping and the clock ticking away. Must have been late afternoon when Caleb strode into the kitchen and called from the bottom of the stairs. "You seen Willy?"

What did he mean, asking me if I'd seen Willy? I set the wool aside and walked to the top of the stairs. "Not since our noon meal," I answered. "He's *supposed* to be with you and Pa. Don't tell me you've gone and lost him."

"He ain't lost. Ruff took off after a rabbit, and Willy went chasing after him. Wasn't but a short time ago. They was heading this way."

"Caleb, how many times do you have to be told that 'ain't' isn't a proper word?" I scolded. "Aunt Margaret is sure enough going to be shocked to hear you talk that way. Willy may have been headed in this direction, but I sure haven't seen him."

"Don't need to worry yourself over how I talk, Hannah. You must be about the bossiest critter in the Utah Territory! And Pa says if Willy *ain't* here, you need to be out looking for him. Him and me are busy with the irrigating." Before I could protest or say more about his atrocious English, he stomped across the kitchen and slammed out the door.

Not more than two months ago, I was getting a tongue-lashing for letting Willy slip away. Now, when Pa failed to watch him, I was the one expected to go off hunting for him. Didn't hardly seem fair, but Pa wouldn't take kindly to hearing my complaint.

"I'll help you look for him. I won't mind getting away from the wool for a spell," said Nellie. "Lots of places around here for a dog to chase after rabbits." We went out and called, but there was no answer.

Followed by Nellie, I hurried to the Santa Rosa and searched along the bank. There was no sign Willy or Ruff had been there, but as I looked at the water surging along, splashing over the rocks, a shudder ran through me. Nellie turned away from the creek. "Let's look up along the foothills. A rabbit would likely go that way." She was right, but I had to search by the water first. I wasn't able to escape the memory of Sally Richmond.

Pa had planted fruit trees and grapes vines on terraced land that sloped up behind our fields where the soil was good and there was less danger of flooding. Behind the trees was a ridge of red rock. A seep on the ridge provided water for the orchard.

A ways west of the orchard, the ridge was broken by a dry creek bed, or dry wash, that led into a narrow, rocky canyon.

We searched along the base of the ridge and soon found paw marks and footprints in the dusty, red dirt. "They're sure enough headed for the wash," I said. "Can't be anyone but Ruff and Willy made these tracks. You go on back to the house. I'll find them. Pa will be coming in to start on the chores, so you best get the potatoes peeled for supper." I didn't envy Nellie that job. The potatoes in the root cellar had begun to shrivel and sprout.

As I followed the tracks toward the wash, the afternoon sun beat down on me. I used a corner of my apron to wipe the sweat from my face. I'd left my bonnet hanging on a peg by the door, and I could almost feel the freckles popping out. As I turned up the wash, each step raised a small cloud of red dust that sifted up over my shoes. Then my skirt caught on the sharp barb of a wolfberry bush.

"Willy York," I grumbled, "every time I go hunting for you, I end up with a basket full of mending." After the scolding he got last time, I didn't expect he'd run off again. Likely the hope of catching himself a pet crowded out all thought of consequences. I didn't much want to see his face when he found out what Ruff had in mind for the rabbit. He'd surely be heartbroken.

At first the trail followed a gentle slope but grew steeper as it passed between red cliffs decked out with gray-green sage and yellow cliff roses. I stopped to catch my breath and admire the beauty, for it was hard to ignore. I stood there and called., but there was no answer. Must be they'd been gone longer than Caleb had let on.

Then, as I was about to start back up the hill, a dry rustling sound set my heart to racing. It came from a stand of mesquite trees no more than three feet from where I stood. A rattler! Out of the corner of my eye, I saw something move. A scream caught in my throat, and I was about to leap away down the steep incline, but a quick glance back stopped me. I trembled with relief. A gray squirrel was scampering about in last year's dry leaves.

Although it had about scared me out of my skin, I was grateful to the squirrel, for it reminded me there was danger on this rocky hillside. Nearby, a sturdy limb hung from a dead tree, just what I needed for protection. Only a bit of bark held it in place. I twisted, pulled, yanked—and when it broke loose, sat down hard on the rocky ground.

"Ding dang it," I mumbled as I struggled to my feet, then armed with the stick, trudged on up the slope following the trail left by Ruff and Willy.

As the minutes dragged by, my throat tightened and I had to fight back tears. I should have found them by now. Why had Pa let him run off like that? He was just a little boy. I was soon gasping for breath as I hurried on up the steep slope. And then somewhere ahead, a dog barked. It had to be Ruff. I was both relieved and annoyed. "Just wait till I get my hands on you Willy York, running off after a rabbit," I mumbled as I hurried on past a stand of junipers. Minutes later, my exasperation changed to fear, and my heart turned to ice. The snarling scream of a mountain lion echoed off the rocks .

Now I ran and stumbled up the steep slope, past an outcropping of gray rock, past a scraggly pinion. The frantic barking grew louder, and the cat screamed again. My foot slipped on the loose rocks. As I fell, sharp gravel gouged my knees and hands. The stick slipped from my grasp and rolled toward the precipice. I couldn't lose it! Just before it tumbled down the hillside, I lunged and grabbed it. Scrambling to my feet, I rushed on up the hill. "Willy!" I screamed, praying that he would answer.

"Hurry, Hannah! Bring the gun!" he yelled.

Relief swept over me at the sound of his voice, but it lasted only a moment. As I rounded a bend in the trail, the scene before me burned into my mind. Willy stood with his back to a tumble of rocks. Ruff stood in front of him, rust fur bristling, lips pulled back in a snarl. A tawny cat crouched on a ledge, ears against its head, long, curved teeth exposed. It screamed and launched itself off the rock shelf.

It all happened in an instant. Ruff rushed the cat. A powerful paw sent him tumbling and yelping in pain. Then the lion was on him, ripping with its claws and sharp fangs. There was a blur of tan and rust fur, screeching snarls and howls of agony. And blood. Willy screamed and cussed as he threw rocks with a strength born of fury.

Yelling with all the breath I had left, I ran forward, lifted the stick in the air and brought it down again and again on the back of the lion. It released its grip on Ruff, turned with a snarl, and swiped at me with bared claws. The white fur around its mouth was red with blood. I swung the stick back and forth in front of it. Finally it turned and streaked off into the trees.

Willy ran to Ruff and knelt beside him. "It's all right, boy. He's gone now." Ruff tried to lift his head. He made a soft whimpering sound and then lay still. "Go get Pa," Willy pleaded. "He can fix 'im." He cradled Ruff's head in his lap and patted him gently. Blood soaked his overalls. Then he burst into tears. "You've got to get Pa," he sobbed.

I sat down beside him and wrapped my arm around his shoulder. Tears stung my eyes. "You need to come with me. The lion might come back." He shook his head. I could tell that he had no intention of leaving Ruff. I didn't know what to do. I had called Ruff a mangy brown dog, a cowardly dog. He stood up to the mountain lion. He was no coward. The minutes dragged on as we sat there sorrowing together. Then I heard Pa calling.

Nellie must have sent him.

"We're here!" I answered.

He came around the bend and stopped for an instant, then he was kneeling by us, a look of horror on his face. "Oh, dear Lord, help us," he prayed.

All that blood. He must have thought we were near dead. Willy looked up into his eyes, as hiccuping sobs shook his body. "Pa, Ruff's hurt bad. You can fix him up, can't you?" he pleaded.

Pa touched my shoulder and his hand shook. "Hannah, are you and Willy hurt?"

"No, just Ruff." Skinned knees didn't seem to be worth mentioning.

His large hands were gentle as he checked Ruff's wounds and felt for a heart beat. Then he slowly shook his head. "Can't anything be done. He's gone. What happened?"

"That damn old mountain lion!" Willy sobbed.

Pa seemed not to hear Willy's description of the cat. He turned to me, and I couldn't stop the tears from rolling down my cheeks. "You don't have to say it, Pa. I should have shot it when I had the chance."

Chapter 11

Pa fixed up a sling. Then he and Caleb carried Ruff off of the mountain so's we could bury him. Pa wanted to bury him up there and tried to convince Willy that it was a fitting place for a dog's grave with junipers and sage and a red rock for a headstone, but Willy put up such a fuss that they brought him down. He said it was too lonely on the hill. Seems I'm not the only one who gives in to his wishes.

We buried him under the apple tree out back. It had been his favorite spot for napping on a hot summer day. Willy insisted we have a regular funeral with a song and prayer. He even persuaded me to give the eulogy. 'Course he didn't call it a eulogy. He just told me to say what a good dog Ruff was. I don't know why he picked me. I'd sure enough said some mean things about Ruff in the past.

When Pa found us by the rock ledge, I'd seen his gentle side that had been missing for so long. It was terrible of me to think it, but he seemed to sorrow more at Ruff's death than he did when Ma died. Most likely though, the sorrow was for Willy. Pa thought the funeral might ease Willy's grief, but night after night he cried out in his sleep, haunted by the mountain lion. I'd get up and hold him, same as I had done after Ma died. Seems it brought comfort to the both of us.

One night as I sat rocking him, Willy look up at me. "Hannah, don't tell Pa about them words I said when the lion was hurting Ruff. He'd likely give me a licking."

"Couldn't anyone blame you for saying what you did. Where'd you ever hear those cuss words anyway?" I asked.

"Over at the livery stable in Brockton. Elbert Hicks said 'em when his old mule up and kicked 'im. I knew they was bad, 'cause Pa said he'd tan me good if he ever heard me talk like that."

I could scarcely believe he'd remembered that string of curses. Must have been saving 'em for a time when they were needed. "I won't tell," I assured him. "But best you never say them again."

It had been a month since we'd received the letter from Aunt Margaret. Shouldn't be long till the stage brought her to Brockton. Pa had arranged with Brother Whitlock to see that she got to the farm. I couldn't help but wonder if our lives would change when she arrived. She hadn't said how long she planned to stay. Nellie was still convinced that she was out to marry Pa. Guess we'd soon find out what kind of woman was coming to live in our house.

Pa hadn't said much, just that we'd best get the place in order for her arrival. I gave Caleb a bucket and sent him for sand so's we could scrub the floors. When he set the bucket on the porch, I handed him the rag rug. "Give this a good beating. Then you can start scrubbing over by the window."

"Don't see why I should be washing floors. It's women's work," he grumbled.

"Until Aunt Margaret gets here, there's no woman around to do it, so you'll just have to help Nellie and me." I was sorry as soon as I'd said it. I didn't need to be reminding them that Ma was gone. And somehow I couldn't picture Aunt Margaret down on her knees scrubbing.

Fitted out with sand, a pig-bristle brush, and a pail of soap suds, we started scouring the floor. "Make sure you clean under the table and benches," I ordered. "Don't want any gobs of dried up food left there."

Caleb scowled. "I don't need you telling me how to scrub."

One thing about Caleb, he worked mighty fast when he was mad. I'd just have to trust that he was getting all the dirt. It wouldn't be wise to vex him more.

When we finished scrubbing, I let the floor dry, then swept the sand out. With the rug back in place, the room looked right nice. I meant to thank Caleb for his help, but he had already gone out to look after the sheep—a chore that was a good deal easier than scrubbing and, more important to my brother, men's work.

Nellie sat on the bench with her elbow on the table, chin propped in her hand. "Once we get the windows washed and clean curtains hung, shouldn't anyone complain about our housekeeping. I just hope Aunt Margaret gets here while the house is still clean. Doesn't take those boys but a few days to track up the floor."

We poured some vinegar in a bucket of water, same as Ma used to do, and washed the windows, Nellie on the inside and me out. I was cleaning the upstairs windowpanes from the drying porch when Pa rode into the lane, stirring up a cloud of red dust. He leaped off of Dan's back, dashed into the house and out again before I had time to wring out the wash rag. When he came out, he was carrying his gun.

"Pa, what's wrong?" I called. The sight of the gun set my heart to thumping.

As he climbed back on his horse, he looked up and saw me. "Caleb found cougar tracks out by the sheep corral. Can't afford to lose any lambs. I'd best see if I can hunt it down before it causes more trouble." His words faded as he galloped away.

I'd secretly hoped to be the one to kill that mountain lion, but I'd be glad just to have it gone. If I had known the grief it would cause, I wouldn't have missed. I'd have aimed to kill—or given the gun to Caleb.

Round about five o'clock, the afternoon sun reflected off

our clean windows. Dinner was cooking, but Pa wasn't back, so Caleb and Willy came for the milk buckets.

"See that you wipe your feet," I called.

"Don't need you to tell me. You think I don't know the floor just got a scrubbing? Clean off your feet, Willy," mocked Caleb. "We don't want to dirty up Hannah's floor."

With Pa gone, the boys would have to do all the evening chores. Nellie offered to help, and the three of them walked off toward the barn. As I set the table, I wished they'd asked me to help. The house was clean, the beans and ham gave off a savory aroma, but I couldn't shake off a feeling of melancholy. Caleb and I never laughed anymore, just snapped at each other like a couple of magpies battling over scraps. And Pa seemed to have his feelings bottled up somewhere inside him. Through all the hard times, we'd been happy. I'd trusted God. Then he took Ma and Jenny. When they died, I lost more than a mother and sister.

An hour later, supper was over, and Pa still wasn't back. Nellie and I went out to weed and water the flowers. The orange sun dropped behind the mountains turning the sky the colors of a ripe peach. It was a pleasant time of day with a breeze bringing relief from the heat of the afternoon. "It's not going to be light much longer," said Nellie as she pulled a chickweed out of the moist soil. "Seems Pa should be back by now."

An uneasy feeling had been growing in me, but I didn't want to worry her. "Can't tell how far he's had to track that lion."

"Must be quite some distance or we'd have heard shooting," said Nellie.

"He could have lost the trail and hasn't had anything to shoot at. Might be, he's trying to pick up the tracks again." This was likely what had happened, but I'd feel a lot better when Pa rode up the lane.

By the time we'd finished our weeding, the sky was a deep lavender. The ghost of a full moon hovered near the eastern hills. Pa had been gone for hours. *Why wasn't he back?*

We walked together to the porch where Nellie and I removed our shoes. Wouldn't hurt none to set an example for the boys to follow. They sat at the table playing checkers. Caleb was trying to teach Willy the rules. I could tell right off Willy was having more fun than Caleb. He jumped his red piece three spaces forward and gleefully removed a black checker.

"Willy, I keep telling you, you can only move one space! It's time to put the checkers away." Caleb ignored Willy's protests as he dropped the red and black discs into their bag. "It's time for you to go to bed."

"I want to wait for Pa and hear about the lion." Willy turned to me. "Can I Hannah?"

"We don't know when Pa will be back. If you're still awake, he can come up and tell you all about it," I promised.

"Pa always reads," he reminded me. I sighed and lit another oil lamp. Willy climbed in Pa's big cushioned chair with me, and we opened our book of Fairy Tales. When I'd finished the story and tucked Willy in bed, I picked up some mending, and we huddled in the dim light cast by the lamps, Nellie knitting, Caleb holding a copy of *Robinson Crusoe* in front of him. But his eyes were on the door, not the book. No one considered going to bed. We sat there, straining to hear hoof beats that would mean Pa was home.

"Thought I heard a shot not long after supper," said Caleb. "Pa's likely skinning that old cat right now."

Neither of us answered. The mantle clock ticked away the minutes. I couldn't keep my mind on the mending. I found I'd caught the front of Pa's overalls as I stitched a patch on the back. I pulled the stitches out, tears stinging my eyes.

"Where is he! Doesn't he know we'd be worried? He better *not* be out there skinning that animal!" I said.

"Then where is he?" whispered Nellie. A tear ran down her tanned cheek.

I could sit still no longer. I went to the door and peered out into the yard. The night was bathed in moonlight. An owl hooted. Then it was quiet except for the burbling sound of water from the creek. No matter how hard I stared, I couldn't make Pa appear out of the shadows. I closed the door and walked over to the mantle. It was nearly midnight. What should I do? I thought to pray, but God and I didn't seem to be on the best of terms lately.

The ticking seemed to grow louder in the silent house. I wanted to stop the clock. Stop it from reminding me of the time that had passed since Pa rode off to hunt the mountain lion.

Then suddenly Caleb jumped up. "Listen! I think I hear a horse coming."

Nellie strained forward, listening. "I hear it too. Pa's back!" She laughed as tears streamed down her face.

Caleb threw the door open, and the sound of hooves thudding on the dirt track grew louder. "Pa! Pa!" we yelled as we ran toward the road. The horse whinnied and trotted around the bend. Even in the shadows cast by the cottonwoods, I recognized Dan by the white blaze on his face.

"Pa—" I started to call to him, but the words died in my throat, and I felt like I'd been hit in the stomach. The saddle was empty.

Chapter 12

We stood for a moment, stunned into silence. Nellie put her hand over her mouth and grabbed my arm. "Pa!" she cried. Sobs shook her body. "Where's Pa?"

Cursing the mountain lion, Caleb grabbed the reins as Dan skittered and snorted. His chestnut coat, wet with sweat, glistened in the moonlight.

"I've got to find him," I said.

"I don't want you to go, too," sobbed Nellie.

"Could be he's lying hurt somewhere." I didn't want to think that he might be dead. Please, not that, I prayed.

"Be best if I go," said Caleb. "A girl shouldn't ride out there at night."

"No, you stay with Nellie and Willy. The whole thing's my fault, not shooting that cat when I had the chance." My voice shook, but I wouldn't let myself cry. "You'll need to take care of Dan. Looks like he's been running hard. I'll ride Dolly."

He nodded his head, and we hurried toward the barn. Good thing he didn't argue. He'd be right annoyed if I had to remind him that I could ride every bit as well as he could.

We saddled Dolly. Then Caleb ran to the house and returned with Ma's old school bell, the one she'd used to call us from the fields. He wrapped it in a feed sack and handed it to me. "Stick this in the saddle bag. If you need me, ring it. I'll be listening."

I nodded, then gave him a hug. There were tears in his eyes, but he turned away so I wouldn't see. Nellie handed me a shawl, threw her arms around me, and squeezed like she thought I was never coming back. It wasn't me I was worried about—it was Pa.

I climbed on Dolly, and nudged her into a trot. When we came to the road, I turned her toward the west, the direction Pa had taken when he rode away. Best chance I had for finding him would be to follow the tracks Dan had left as he fled for home—if he had left hoof prints I could follow with only the moon to light the way. I pulled back on the reins and slowed Dolly to a walk. It wouldn't matter how fast I rode unless I knew where Pa had been. Moonlight illuminated the ground. As I peered ahead, I could see Dan's tracks in the soft dirt. Must have been the first time I'd thought kindly of that red dust. From the spacing of the hoof prints, I figured he'd been moving at a full gallop.

I was pleased with my tracking skills until I suddenly realized the tracks in the dusty road had disappeared. I pulled Dolly to a stop. Must be I'd missed the spot where Dan galloped onto the road from the field. I turned and back-tracked until I found faint hoof marks in the rocky, sage-covered ground. I felt a knot in my stomach. The tracks were coming from the direction of the red-rock ridge. I guess I knew all along that was where the trail would lead—up the dry wash to the place where I'd last seen the tawny cat. I nudged Dolly ahead and followed Dan's tracks.

The full moon caste an eerie light on the desert ground. This familiar land appeared new and enchanted. Strange shadows, rocks, and brush made it hard to follow Dan's trail, but I felt as though I were being pulled to the opening in the ridge that led up the narrow canyon. I figured the cat must live in a cave in the rocks. I soon grew restless, weaving back and forth through the brush, straining to see hoof prints. I urged Dolly into a slow trot, not daring to go faster for fear she'd stumble in a gopher hole, and headed straight for the dry wash.

I felt sure I'd be able to pick up the trail at the mouth of the narrow canyon.

A strong smell of sage filled the night air. From somewhere in the distance, a coyote howled. I shivered as a cool breeze blew up from the river bottom.

I thought of Caleb and Nellie sitting at home, sick with worry. I hoped they were sleeping, but Caleb had promised to listen for the bell, and he sure enough wouldn't go back on a promise. I was grateful I was here on Dolly's back, not pacing and waiting at home. Ma called me her impatient child, always sneaking down the stairs on Christmas Eve before the presents were out. Maybe that's why Caleb didn't argue with me tonight. He knew I never could stand to sit and wait for anything.

When I reached the mouth of the narrow canyon, I dismounted and wrapped the reins around a mesquite branch. While sitting astride Dolly's broad back, breathing in her familiar smell and touching her rough mane and smooth neck, I'd felt safe. Now standing on my own two feet, that feeling of safety was gone, but I would need to look closely for tracks. I sure enough didn't want to go riding up that wash unless I found signs that Dan had been there. Doubts had begun to creep into my head. Had I been foolish to follow my hunch instead of hoof marks?

I searched the mouth of the dry wash from rock wall to rock wall and back again. There was no sign that a horse had been there. A sick feeling overwhelmed me, and I began to cry. I had to find Pa. In my haste, I'd wasted precious time. I had been so sure I knew where Dan's tracks would lead me.

As I went back to Dolly and loosed the reins, she snorted and nuzzled my shoulder as if to comfort me. I leaned against her warm side. I had to calm down, take time to think. I was sure Dan had been running from someplace along the ridge of red rock. If he had been east of the wash, he would have taken a trail by the orchard, so Pa must have followed the cat farther west. If I rode slowly along the base of the ridge, I should run across tracks near the next gap in the rock wall, the gap folks called Kaboti Canyon.

The moon had moved to the western sky, and I knew it was late. I leaned forward in the saddle, straining to find Dan's tracks. How long was it since I'd left home? I'd lost track of time, but it must be getting on toward morning. The air had grown chilly. The only sound was the clip clopping of Dolly's hooves. It was just a short distance now to the narrow canyon that cut into the rocky ridge. I felt compelled to hurry, but dreaded what I might find.

I recalled the evening when I had stood by the sheep pen, looking into the yellow eyes of the mountain lion. If only I'd had the sense to shoot him!

Now Ruff was dead, and Pa was. . . "Stop it!" I told myself. "You're going to find him. Everything will be all right." And as I battled my imagination, I rode up to the mouth of Kaboti Canyon.

This time I didn't have to dismount to look for hoof marks. They were there, plain to see. The soft ground was churned up where Pa had ridden into the narrow canyon and Dan had galloped out. Pa must be up there—or could he have ridden out again and then disappeared somewhere in the desert? I dismissed the thought, turned Dolly, and rode ahead into the shadowy canyon where the rock wall cut off light from the moon. Dolly felt her way carefully up the slope, gravel crunching under her hooves. A sudden movement on the right caused her to shy and sent my heart to racing. A deer burst from cover and bounded out of sight.

As we moved up the canyon, rocks dislodged by Dolly's hooves, clattered and slid down behind us. Then we rounded a bend, and I saw him. "Pa!" I screamed. I slid off of Dolly and ran to where he lay, crumpled next to a rock fall. Dry blood had matted his hair and blotched the ground. Numb with fear, I sat down and lifted his head onto my lap.

"Pa? Please answer me, Pa," I pleaded. Tears ran down my cheeks.

He opened his eyes and relief swept over me. He was alive! "Hannah, is that you?" he mumbled. "What are you doing here? You should be fixing supper." His words were slurred, then his eyes closed. Fixing supper? The bump must had sent him out of his head.

"I came to find you," I whispered. "You've got to get on Dolly's back." I tried to help him up, but he moaned and made no effort to rise. What could I do? I had to get him home. I ran to the saddle bag, grabbed Ma's bell and shook it till my arm felt near to falling off. The deep clanging echoed off the canyon walls, but I feared I was too far from home for Caleb to hear. I wrapped Nellie's shawl around him, sat down by his side and waited, hoping he would soon regain his senses. Every little while, I got up and rang the bell in hopes Caleb would hear, and the sound would lead him to us.

I sat there surrounded by silence as the night edged toward dawn. My eyes closed and my head began to droop, but I jerked up fully awake as I became aware of a familiar sound—the clatter of rocks as a horse moved up the rocky trail. He had heard the bell! I jumped up and yelled, "Caleb, we're here!"

Then my heart leaped into my throat, and in an instant my joy turned to fear. It wasn't Caleb who came around the bend. In the dim light I saw the outline of three mounted Indians. I couldn't run, and I dared not scream. I just stood there, hardly breathing.

Chapter 13

One of the Indians dismounted and walked toward me. His thick, dark hair hung down in braids. "My people hear bell. Chief Chuarumpeak send Saugawa. Him say go see what matter. I come." Then he walked over and knelt by Pa. "Him hurt in head. Saugawa help."

My knees were wobbly, but the terror had faded. These Indians were not a part of Black Hawk's band. Saugawa had been to our farm to trade—and Pa had called him a friend. I don't rightly know why, but I broke down and cried like a baby.

Saugawa tended to Pa's wounds and gave him water to drink. He spoke to one of the braves who rode off down the canyon. "Him bring Indian medicine. Good for head. You father, him sleep much. Be better soon."

Then they helped Pa onto a horse and we left Kaboti Canyon.

We rode up to the house just after dawn. Caleb came running to meet us as we turned up the lane. He must have been listening through the night, waiting for the sound of the bell or hoof beats on the road. His brown eyes were red-rimmed, his face pale as we helped Pa off of the horse and up to the house. Nellie had fallen asleep but woke when the door opened. She ran to him, buried her head on his chest, and sobbed. He patted her head and whispered, "It's all right, Nell. Everything's going to be all right."

Saugawa said Pa would sleep much, and he did. He slept all day and through the night, and most of the next day and night, rousing only when we brought him water, soup, and the Indian medicine. The four of us were about tuckered out, what with looking after Pa and the farm, too. The weather had turned hot and dry, so water from the creek had to be diverted to water the garden. With the mountain lion roaming about and no dog to keep watch, we had moved the sheep into the fenced field near the barn and hoped they'd be safe.

On Monday morning, Pa woke up, surprised that he felt so weak. He was confused and didn't remember much that had happened after riding out after the mountain lion on Friday. When I told him where I'd found him, he recalled following cougar tracks into the shadowy canyon and reaching back for his gun. The cat had snarled and Dan reared. After that, he remembered little. He had no idea how long he'd been sleeping or what day it was. When we told him it was Monday, he was upset that he'd slept through church.

About nine o'clock, Brother Whitlock rode into the yard. He had been concerned when we missed the Sunday meetings. After listening to Pa's story, he offered to send Charles up with Henry and their dog Tag. Tag could watch the sheep, and Henry, who was Caleb's age, could stay for a few days to help with chores till Pa got his strength back. Caleb was right happy with the arrangement. As for me, I could scarcely hide my pleasure. Charles would be bringing them! I'd invite him for supper before he returned home.

The next morning though, it was Bishop Crawford who drove up with Henry and the sheep dog. He was taking his sister Annie and her six-year-old daughter to St. George, and since he'd be passing by our place, he'd offered to save Charles a trip. Although I'm fond of the bishop and his sister, my heart about dropped down to my toes when I realized his generosity meant I'd not see Charles. I greeted them with a weak smile and hoped my disappointment didn't show, while the rest of the family welcomed them with obvious pleasure.

It couldn't have been a pleasant trip for Annie and Sarah,

sharing the two hour wagon ride with Tag. I reckon he'd been breathing down their necks most of the way. When the wagon stopped, he leaped over the side-board and ran sniffing around the yard. When he bounded back to where we stood, Sarah hid behind her mother's skirt.

Willy held out his hand, "Here, boy. Good dog." Tag bared his teeth and growled. Willy's lower lip turned down as he pulled back his hand in surprise.

"Don't worry. He won't hurt ya," said Henry. "He just has to get to know ya."

But Tag had missed his chance to get to know Willy, who from that moment on refused to have anything to do with him. Must have been the first animal that Willy didn't take a liking to. Sarah, who shared this animosity, became Willy's friend.

I'd looked forward to eating our noon meal with Charles, but instead we shared it with Bishop Crawford and Annie Thornton. She had lost the haggard look that I remembered from that day at the cemetery just a little more than a month ago. The dark circles under her blue eyes were gone, and her light brown hair was pulled back in a bun. It was good to see her smile as she and the bishop visited with Pa.

You'd think we lived in town what with all the people traveling down our road of late. The following Wednesday in the heat of the afternoon, Aunt Margaret arrived with all her baggage. Caleb called when he heard a wagon rattling down the dusty road. We met them as the horses turned into the yard. Aunt Margaret sat stiff and straight on the wagon seat next to Charles. She wore a brown silk traveling dress with a high lace collar, its beauty marred by a layer of dust, wrinkles, and perspiration stains. Strands of damp hair had escaped from under her brown velvet hat and hung down on her neck and flushed face. Her light red hair was the color of Ma's, but her lips pressed together in a tight line and the sharp features were hers alone.

While the rest of us stood staring and speechless, Pa stepped forward to help her down from the wagon. "Welcome to our farm, Margaret. We've been looking forward to your arrival. Must have been a long hot trip. Come sit in the shade. You must be needing a cool drink of water."

"Thank you, Isaac, but I'm quite capable of getting down by myself, and what I'm needing is a bath. I don't suppose you have a bath tub."

"Of late, we been taking our baths in the rinsing trough down by the sheep pens. You could bath there," offered Willy.

"Saves hauling water," added Caleb. 'We hang up a blanket for privacy, and ain't no one around going to see ya." .

"Isn't anyone around," she corrected.

"Nope! Not for miles," said Willy.

Wasn't many could resist Willy's charms, and a faint smile softened her features. With the smile, I saw some small resemblance to Ma, but where Aunt Margaret was tall and bony with a thin face and sharp features, Ma's figure had been filled out, her face rounder, softer.

"Perhaps a basin of water and some soap will do for now," she said. "After experiencing the primitive transportation in this territory, I don't suppose I can expect too much in the way of civilized comforts." I could only guess what her reaction would be to the privy.

I watched as Pa and Charles carried three large trunks into the room that would be Aunt Margaret's. Seemed she must have brought everything she owned. Perhaps Nellie was right, and she did plan to stay and marry Pa. I closed my eyes and prayed fervently that Nell was wrong. Pa had given her his room and moved his things upstairs to one end of the spinning room. At first, I feared Nellie and I would be expected to share our room with her and was relieved to learn otherwise. We would need some time by ourselves, away from her disapproving eyes.

While Aunt Margaret unpacked, I sat down on the porch with Charles. He sighed and shook his head. "I sure don't envy you none. That is the complainingest woman I ever saw. Acted like the dust and bumps were my fault. And I do believe she thought the heat was my doing, too. Said the trip by stage was bad enough, but at least the seats were cushioned and she had some protection from the sun and dust. Guess I should have thought to bring a pillow for her sitting comfort."

"Too bad you were the one had to bring her," I said with fingers crossed.

"Don't worry none about it. Gives me a chance to visit with you and your Pa. Besides, I didn't pay any mind to her complaints. Just said 'Yes, Ma'am' and 'No, Ma'am.'"

Charles wanted to visit me! Well, me and Pa. A feeling of good will came over me, even towards Aunt Margaret. "I'm hoping she may be different when she's rested some. It's been a tiring trip for her."

"How long you reckon she plans to stay?" he asked.

"Looks to be a good while, what with all that baggage she brought."

"Yep, I helped load and unload those trunks, but I wouldn't worry none. I figure she won't stay as long as she planned. She's too highfalutin' for these parts."

We didn't say more, for Aunt Margaret came out onto the porch looking considerably better than she had an hour ago. She stood, hand on hip, and peered down at me. "Seems you could find something useful to do, Hannah. The house looks as though it could use a good cleaning."

I had to clamp my mouth shut to keep the angry words from pouring out. All the scrubbing and polishing we'd done for her arrival! All the work of the last week! How could she say such a thing? When I gained control of my temper, I remembered how Charles had answered her.

"Yes Ma'am," I said and continued to sit there on the porch.

She no doubt would have had more to say, but Willy, Caleb, Henry and Tag came racing around the side of the house. Tag, as usual, seemed to be frothing at the mouth. He greeted Aunt Margaret with bared teeth and a menacing growl. After all, he hadn't gotten to know her. The thought crossed my mind that if he knew her better, he may have bitten her.

"Get that disgusting mongrel away from me!" she ordered.

"We used to have a good dog," said Willy, "but a mountain lion killed 'im."

"Mountain lion! A dangerous animal is roaming around your farm?"

I thought for a moment Aunt Margaret might fall over in a dead faint until I realized it was not an exclamation of fear but one of outrage. I had the feeling there wasn't much could scare Aunt Margaret. She would no doubt stand up to Black Hawk himself.

Chapter 14

Aunt Margaret wasn't one to waste time. The day after arriving, she unpacked a stack of books, set them on the table with a thump, and said she was going to teach us some grammar. I just *knew* she'd disapprove of Caleb's English, and mercy knows I'd done my best to correct it. "Aunt Margaret," I said, "not all of us need grammar lessons."

"There will be ample time for other subjects." Then she looked around and made a tsk-tsking sound. "I can't abide smoke-stained walls. It's well past time for a coat of whitewash. It's plain we'll have to schedule time for some thorough house cleaning as well. And I won't rest easy until all the bedding's been washed. Things have been sorely neglected since your mother died."

Did she think we had cooties? I had to clamp my mouth shut again. If I said what was on my mind, I'd be in a heap of trouble.

Two days later, soon as we'd finished the day's lessons and Caleb had gone to help Pa, she declared it a good time to wash the bedding. We hauled and heated water; then scrubbed, wrung, and hung the quilts and sheets. We were like to collapse with the heat, for it was a hot day to begin with. Aunt Margaret looked as frazzled as she had when she'd arrived in the wagon— the flushed face and damp, drooping hair. Only the dust was missing. We tried to tell her before we started dismantling the beds that we'd washed all the quilts early in the spring when the weather was cool. I thought it was charitable of me not to remind her of that as she sat on the porch fanning herself.

"Nellie and I are thinking to go down to the rinsing trough

for a bath," I told her. She nodded. "Yes, I think a bath would be in order." I didn't figure she'd object, what with cleanliness being so important to her.

We turned the water into the trough same as when we rinsed the fleece, then hung blankets on the lines Pa had strung. While Nellie bathed, I sat in the shade and untied my braids. When it was my turn, I sank down in the cool water and held on to the sides while my hair floated around my head and my body bobbed up and down. This was as close as I ever came to swimming. Caleb taunted me when I refused to join them in the swimming hole, but a deep fear always held me back. My memory of the Platte River was always with me.

When we returned to the house, Aunt Margaret called us to help empty the wash tub she'd used for her bath. She could have saved herself a lot of trouble if she'd done as we had done. It must have been uncomfortable for her in that little tub. I smiled as I imagined her sitting there with her bony knees poking out.

That night during supper, Pa informed Aunt Margaret that school work would have to be done in the evenings. During the growing season, we were all needed in the fields.

"I suppose something can be arranged," she said in her prim way, plainly vexed.

"We'd be right happy to have you ride over and attend church with us tomorrow," said Pa. "It would give you a chance to meet some of our neighbors. I don't like leaving you here alone."

"No thank you, Isaac. I think not. I shall stay here and read my Bible." We ate in silence, the only sound coming from utensils scraping on earthenware plates. Then Aunt Margaret put her fork down, looked disapprovingly at the boys and turned to Pa. "I hope you aren't taking those two to church looking like that. Their hair is a disgrace. I can cut it for them after supper."

I felt like crying as Willy's red curls fell to the floor. They were so like Ma's. When Aunt Margaret was through snipping, I hardly recognized my own brothers. It reminded me somewhat of the day we sheared the sheep.

In the morning, the boys started complaining as soon as they got out of bed. "I'm not going to church till my hair grows back!" said Caleb. "Folks will think I been scalped."

"Everyone will laugh," said Willy. I felt sorry for them, but Pa ignored their complaints. Wouldn't do them any good to put up a fuss. They'd go anyway.

"No one's like to notice your hair," said Pa. He never has paid much mind to appearances. Actually, it would be hard not to notice since there was now a band of white skin where the hair had been.

Their complaints had no effect on Pa. We left early and arrived at the church before ten. Although there where a few snickers, no one dared tease Caleb. He wore a look that warned against it. It was worse for Willy. Maude Winkle sashayed over waving her handkerchief. "Why, Willy dear, whatever has happened to those adorable red curls of yours?"

Willy ducked his head. "Hannah put 'em in a box," he mumbled.

That woman! I took his hand and hurried toward the door. Pa was standing there, talking with Bishop Crawford and Annie Thornton. The way Pa smiled at her gave me an uncomfortable feeling that I tried to ignore. I was being silly. What did I expect him to do—scowl at her? Pa motioned to us to join him, then led us to our usual seats, Pa next to Willy. He hadn't forgotten the lizards.

After the meeting, we joined the Whitlocks at Bishop Crawford's home for dinner. Eliza and I helped in the kitchen, then went out to the shaded porch where Charles had saved us a place. I hoped Caleb wouldn't take notice and decide to tease me, but he was too busy eating cold fried chicken and thick slices of bread.

"How you getting along with your aunt?" asked Charles.

I sighed. "She's not been here a week, and she's already teaching us grammar. On top of that, she insisted we wash all the bedding in the house. It wasn't but two months ago Nellie and I washed the quilts. Now she wants the whole place scrubbed and the walls white-washed."

"Mercy sakes," said Eliza. "Glad she's not my aunt."

"I didn't figured she'd be easy to live with," said Charles.

"Pa told her last night, he needed our help with the fruit harvest. She acted right put out about it. Brought joy to the rest of us though."

"I hope you can get away at the end of fruit season," said Charles. "I was thinking to hike to the waterfall at the top of Black Creek Canyon. Thought you might want to go along. It's something to see. The water tumbles down the rocks into a pool at the bottom. The whole place is green, with ferns growing everywhere. "

I wanted to go, but was compelled to ask, "Is the creek deep?"

"Not this time of year. Come August when your Pa brings his apples and melons to market, it won't be much more than a trickle. You could ride down with him and spend the day. It's a fair hike, but it's worth it."

"We can pack a lunch," said Eliza. Then she looked at Charles. "I guess I'm invited, too."

"I reckon you can come." Then Charles smiled his amazing smile. "Don't reckon her Pa'd allow her to go if you didn't."

I was ready to ask Pa right then, but when I turned around, he was talking with Annie again. They were smiling and laughing. I turned away, feeling like a spy. Somehow I felt jealous—jealous for Ma.

Late in the afternoon, we drove back into the yard, hot and eager to cool off in the shade of the apple tree.

"Come on, Caleb!" yelled Willy. "Let's go change out a these Sunday-meeting clothes so we can stick our feet in the irrigating ditch." The boys raced ahead to the house. They'd just disappeared through the door when I heard Willy yell, "You killed him! Why'd ya do that, Aunt Margaret?" He sounded close to tears. I raced up the path not knowing what I'd find. Aunt Margaret stood there, broom in hand, with a look of triumph on her face. At her feet lay the body of a small gray mouse.

"I was going to catch him for a pet," said Willy as he stooped down to pick up the tiny animal.

"Don't touch that filthy rodent!" screeched Aunt Margaret as she covered it with the broom. "They carry all kinds of nasty diseases and plagues. I'll just sweep him onto the dust pan and get rid of him."

Pa came in and intervened. Ended up with us having another funeral out by the tree where Ruff was buried. We all gathered around to pay our last respects to the mouse—all but Aunt Margaret who refused to attend.

Chapter 15

I'd never seen Caleb so interested in farm work until it freed us from Aunt Margaret's tyranny. Now he could scarcely wait to get out in the fields. All through June, July and into August, Pa needed our help on the farm most every day. What with irrigating, weeding, picking, drying, and preserving—and this on top of our regular chores—work days were long, leaving us little time for grammar.

In the orchard, the apricots ripened first, then it wasn't but a few week till the peaches were ripe. Although Pa traded much of our fruit, we made preserves and dried part of the crop. The peaches were more work than the apricots since they had to be sliced before they were dried. Eliza Whitlock came over and spent two days helping out. It wasn't often I had a friend sleep over. What could have been a chore seemed more like a party as we worked together. Whenever Aunt Margaret started harping at us, Eliza would look at me and raise her eyebrows in an expression of disbelief. Funny how that took the sting out of the nagging.

"I don't see why something as tasty as a peach has to be covered with prickly fuzz." Nellie wiped her hands on her apron. "I itch all over!"

She was rinsing the fruit in a large tub so we could stone and slice it for drying. A layer of fuzz floated on top. Eliza wrinkled up her nose and scratched her arm. "Looks to be time to change the water," she said.

I sighed. "Makes me wish we were still doing apricots."

"If you girls would stop rubbing your arms and faces you wouldn't be bothered by a little peach fuzz. I declare, you spend more time scratching than you do slicing. And don't wipe the juice on your aprons. The stains will never come out." Aunt Margaret was full of advice and always willing to share it.

Despite the fuzz and the sticky juice that ran down our arms, we laughed as we worked. Soon peach slices, arranged on racks and protected by netting, replaced apricots on the drying porch. The dried apricots were stored for winter.

Next, we made peach preserves. When the fruit was washed and sliced, Aunt Margaret put it in a large kettle, added molasses and set it on the brick stove Pa had built on the wash porch. It had a thick iron top to cook on when the weather was hot. It kept the house cooler, but not the cook.

"Aunt Margaret," I said, "I don't think you have to stir all the time while it simmers." I knew that Ma had stirred only enough to keep the preserves from burning.

She harrumphed and continued to stir with the wooden spoon. "I know about cooking peach preserves. I'll not have them scorched."

I offered to take a turn, but she insisted she could do it. I doubt Aunt Margaret had perspired as much in her entire life as she had since coming to the Utah Territory. I was getting accustomed to seeing her with a red face, sweaty brow, damp stains under her arms, and drooping hair.

Nellie and Eliza suggested we go to the trough for a bath, but I said I'd come later. I didn't want Aunt Margaret fainting away with no one there to revive her. Finally she tested a spoonful of preserves and declared them done. I helped her lift the kettle off of the stove and ladle the thick confection into crocks.

She sat down on the bench and wiped her brow. "Thank you, Hannah," she said, "for being so willing to help. I've been thinking—"

She thought for a good long time. Then she continued, "I've

been thinking perhaps I'll try a bath in the rinsing trough. The water is clean, isn't it? And I can count on privacy?"

I nodded. "You'll like it, Aunt Margaret. You'll see. When Nellie and Eliza come back, I'll walk down there with you."

"That won't be necessary. I can find the way." Now she sounded like the same old Aunt Margaret. Just when I thought she might have changed.

Coming in from the field, Pa and the boys found Eliza, Nellie and me sitting on the porch. We told him we'd finished with the preserves and supper was started.

"Where is your aunt?" asked Pa.

Nellie was quick to answer. "You won't believe it! She's down in the rinsing trough taking a bath. She's been there a good long while, too. Hannah's still waiting for her turn."

"We may make a farmer of her yet," said Pa.

I didn't like the sound of that. Nellie poked me in the ribs and gave me a look that said, "I told you so!"

The next morning, Eliza had to leave. I was sad to see her go. Now the work would seem like work again.

With the peaches dried and preserves made, Aunt Margaret declared it was time to clean the house. Caleb was sent for sand to scrub the plank floors. Aunt Margaret said she expected us to do a thorough job, then walked out, leaving us on our knees scrubbing. Caleb scowled as he attacked the floor with the bristle brush. I could tell he was down-right angry about her orders, but for once, I wasn't the object of his resentment. Difference was, he back-talked me, but didn't dare sass Aunt Margaret.

When we'd finished scrubbing, I swept up the sand while Caleb and Nellie sat on the porch. Caleb's words drifted in through the window.

"I sure do wish Aunt Margaret would have a mind to go back to Boston. Never saw anyone could pester a person with so many do's and don'ts. Compared to that woman, Hannah's orders seem right tolerable."

I leaned out the door. "I hope you remember what you just said, Caleb York!"

"Tolerable, not enjoyable," he shot back.

How could he compare me to Aunt Margaret? If he wasn't so contrary, I wouldn't all the time have to be telling him what to do. Right tolerable indeed!

I walked out through the lean-to and over toward the rise where Ma and Jenny were buried near the honey locust tree. I hadn't been there since Christmas. The sun had been shining that day, and it was warm for December. I remembered sitting on the outcropping of rock near the graves, sobbing. I had hoped to gain some comfort there, but felt only sorrow. I hadn't wanted to go back until today.

I climbed up over the rise and stopped, surprised at what I saw. Someone had been there. The weeds were pulled, and a bouquet of flowers had been placed between the graves. Aunt Margaret must have come while we were scrubbing. I felt a stab of guilt, remembering my uncharitable thoughts and words. She'd taken care of Ma's grave, something I should have done. I returned to the house determined to treat her more kindly.

Chapter 16

The next morning, Pa left early to deliver fruit and pick up supplies in St. George. Aunt Margaret, who went along to shop, seemed right pleased about the chance to go to the city, declaring that we were woefully lacking in household supplies. But I think that might have been an excuse for making the trip. In truth, I reckon she was just happy to spend a day away from the farm. I feared she would be disappointed in St. George though. It was nothing like the Boston I had read about.

It hadn't cooled off during the night, and though it wasn't much after seven, the kitchen was sweltering. Caleb and Willy sat dawdling at the table as if it were some kind of holiday. Pa had rattled off a list of chores that needed to be done, and Aunt Margaret added to the list. The way the boys were moving, we'd be lucky to have half of the chores finished by the time they returned.

I wiped my hands on my apron and glared at my brothers. "Morning's about gone, and you two are poking along not half done with breakfast. Sun's going to be blazing down in a few hours, and you'll be telling me it's too hot for weeding."

"Breakfast wasn't much to brag about." Caleb pushed his bowl aside and moved from the table. "Just corn mush and molasses. Ma would've cooked cornbread, maybe even ham. And ya don't need to stand there tapping your foot. I ain't deaf. I heard Pa say to water and weed. Don't need you givin' orders."

I ignored his grammar. Wouldn't do any good to mention it.

Willy slid off the pine bench. "Yeah, Hannah. You don't need to be so bossy."

I turned and faced them. "You know the ham's to be saved for winter. You may be twelve, Caleb York, but sometimes you don't show a bit of sense. Pa expects me to see to things when he's away. I may not like it, but I aim to do it."

"Should be easy for a fine big girl like you," he sneered. "And you're sounding more like Aunt Margaret every day."

I felt my face burn as Caleb mimicked Maude Winkle. "*Such a fine big girl. Must be most as tall as your Pa.*" Her words echoed in my ears. I despised that woman! And I most certainly didn't sound like Aunt Margaret. Or did I? I gritted my teeth, grabbed a pail and strode out to the pump.

As I set the water on the brick stove to heat for the wash, Nellie touched my arm. "Don't pay any mind to them boys. They're just mad 'cause they couldn't go with Pa."

Caleb paused at the door and aimed a scowl in my direction. "I'm riding Dolly up the creek to divert the water. Will can start on the weeds."

"What about Indians?" asked Willy. "Remember what they done to Sarah's pa? Tom Barker says they been stealing cattle around these parts."

"Tom's always stirring up trouble. Besides, he was talking about Black Hawk's renegades. Only Indians near here are a friendly band of Paiutes. No Indians are going to bother you." I handed Willy a hat. "Take this. Isn't any room between those freckles now."

I stood by the door, watching as he trudged toward the garden. Nellie joined me and leaned her head on my shoulder. "I miss Ma. Must be worse for Willy, him just nearing six."

I nodded. "He looks a lot like her, red hair and all. Nellie, you don't think I'm sounding like Aunt Margaret, do you?"

"'Course not. You just sound like yourself," she said.

Somehow her answer did little to comfort me.

The July sun had climbed the sky and the wash room sweltered in its glare. I wiped sweat from my forehead, hung the scrub board up, and rubbed my back. "It's taken almost all morning, but the washing's finally done. Never took Ma near so long."

"We ought to have a picnic, seeing's how we've worked so hard," said Nellie.

"Did you forget? There's cream waiting to be—" I didn't finish. The door banged open, and the boys rushed in.

"Indians, Hannah! I told you there were Indians!" gasped Willy.

"They're not from around here, and they ain't acting the least bit friendly!" Caleb barred the door. "They've turned their horses into the alfalfa. They asked for Pa. Willy told them he's gone for supplies."

"Oh no! You told them Pa's gone? No telling what they'll do now." I peered through the window and saw two braves walking toward the barn. Another was in the field ripping corn from the stalks. Four Indian ponies trampled the alfalfa.

"Can't let them take our corn and ruin the hay. We can't make it through the winter if they do. 'Course, if they take the animals, won't be a need for hay." Caleb reached for Pa's rifle.

I put my hand on his shoulder. "No! A gun won't help. Maybe get us killed."

"I didn't mean to tell that Pa was away." Willy burst into tears.

I put an arm around him. "Don't cry. You didn't know."

Nellie pressed against me sobbing. The memory of the Thorntons lying dead behind the livery stable flashed across my mind. I couldn't let them hurt my family! I had to do something. I'd heard talk in town that some Indians will bully you if you're weaker and they know you're scared.

"They're going to think Pa's come home a lot sooner than expected!" I said. Grabbing his gray homespun shirt from a peg, I pulled it on. "Quick, Nellie! Get some of Ma's hairpins and combs. Help me pin up my hair so's Pa's hat will cover it! Caleb, where did you tie Dolly?"

"Side of the house by the lilac bush."

"Good! Can you get her 'round back without being seen?"

As Caleb nodded and dashed out the lean-to, I wriggled into a pair of Pa's overalls.

"Hannah, what you gonna do?" asked Willy.

"You'll see." My heart raced as Nellie pinned up my braids and handed me Pa's old felt hat. I grabbed a piece of charcoal out of the fireplace and rubbed it around my jaw.

"How's that?" I asked, hoping a smile would hide my fear.

Nellie stepped back and observed the transformation. "You look just like Pa—well, almost."

"I aim to give those Indians a surprise! Mind what Caleb says while I'm gone." I grabbed the rifle and went out the back where he waited with Dolly.

"I'll ride through the orchard, then along the ridge until I can cut across the fields to the creek. I aim to come back on the road so they'll think Pa's back from town. Shouldn't take me long. Hope those renegades don't look too close. Stay in the house and keep the doors bolted. If they try to break in, hide in the root cellar."

"Maybe you shouldn't," he said, but he helped me onto Dolly's back. I didn't answer, just nudged the mare with my knees and bending low, rode toward the orchard.

Sweat ran down my neck. My spine tingled. I'd be in the open until I reached the apple trees. Grasshoppers buzzed in the dry grass. A meadowlark called—and then I was there, surrounded by the smell of ripe fruit.

Ducking under limbs, I moved carefully through the trees.

A sharp branch raked my face and threatened to rip Pa's hat away. When I reached the far end of the orchard, I followed the ridge, then nudged Dolly into a gallop and raced toward the cottonwoods lining the Santa Rosa Creek.

I urged her through the shallow water that trickled around rocks in the near-dry stream bed, then up past the willows to dry, sage-covered ground. Rocks and gopher holes made speed impossible. It was taking too long. I gritted my teeth in frustration. What was happening at home? When I rode into the yard, could I yell like Pa, or would my voice betray me?

In the sagebrush something moved. The dry rustling sound of a diamondback pierced the silence. Dolly reared, then broke into a gallop. With jaws clenched, I pulled back on the reins, trusting that no gopher hole would trip us since she wasn't about to slacken her pace.

We fairly flew across the rough ground. Then through the cottonwoods, I saw the bridge. I turned Dolly onto the road and raced toward home. When the farm was in sight, I slowed her to a canter. With throat dry and hands shaking, I gripped the reins. "Please God," I pleaded, "I need your help." After all my doubting, I had little hope that he'd listen.

As Dolly trotted into the yard, I saw the Indians by the barn loading Pa's wagon with corn and watermelons. Did they mean to take the farm wagon, too? Indignation replaced my fear. "What's going on here?" I bellowed.

"Come trade pine nut for melon," came the harsh reply.

"Get those horses out of my alfalfa and put the nuts by the shed." I held up my fingers. "Four melons." My body trembled, but my voice was steady and deep.

A tall brave walked toward me. "Oh, please," I prayed, "don't let him come closer."

He stopped ten feet away. "Corn?" he asked.

"No corn. Just melons." I sat as tall as I could astride Dolly with Pa's hat tilting forward concealing my face and with my hand on Pa's rifle. I knew if I got down, my legs would crumple and I'd land in a heap at his feet.

The brave stood staring at me while my heart drummed in my chest. Then he signaled to the others who turned, rounded up their horses, collected the melons, and rode toward the fence. They were forgetting the pine nuts.

"Put the nuts by the shed!" I ordered. *What had compelled me to say that?* Perhaps I *had* become as bossy as Aunt Margaret.

The tall brave turned back, and oh, how I wished I'd said nothing. But he rode straight to the shed and dropped a bulging bag. Then he rejoined the others and they galloped out of the yard. A cloud of dust settled behind them as they disappeared down the road.

Trembling and weak, I slid off of Dolly's back and collapsed onto the patch of lawn by the lilac bush. With eyes closed, I uttered a prayer of thanks.

The door opened a crack, and Caleb peered out. Then they were at my side.

"You fooled them!" Nellie threw her arms around me. "We heard. You sounded a mighty lot like Pa!"

"Must'a been easy seeing as how she's been practicing on us for the good part of a year," said Caleb, but his eyes betrayed his gruff tone, and I saw the hint of a smile.

Willy ran off toward the shed. "Think I'll go get them pine nuts." He brought the bag back and struggled with the rawhide tie. As he opened it, his face fell. "Golly, Hannah, they tricked us. Isn't nothing but rocks and straw!"

"Well, I'm sure not going to go chasing after them. It's worth a few watermelons to have them gone."

Caleb pointed to the wagon. "Besides, Pa's going to be mighty pleased we got all that corn picked. 'Course, that means there's some shuckin' to be done later."

"Then we might as well have us a picnic now." Nellie grinned. "Watermelon's picked. Be a shame to waste it."

"You know, Hannah," said Caleb, "it's lucky you're such a fine big girl."

I gave him a shove, and for the first time in months, we sat there by the lilac bush and laughed together.

Chapter 17

Late in the evening, we heard clomping hooves as the wagon rattled into the yard and knew Pa and Aunt Margaret were back. She bustled in, loaded down with packages, informing us that Pa would bring the rest in shortly.

"I'm afraid the stores in Saint George are woefully lacking when it comes to the latest merchandise." To hear Aunt Margaret tell it, the entire west was woefully lacking in one thing or another. Then she added, "I did find some muslin that will be satisfactory for new curtains." She unwrapped a package of yellow cotton, smiling as she held it up for our inspection. "I can't abide old faded curtains against newly whitewashed walls. We'll start them right away."

"Oh, Aunt Margaret, it's beautiful!" exclaimed Nellie. "The curtains will match our yellow daisies. With a bouquet of them on the table, the kitchen will look right cheerful."

The next package contained store-bought suits and white shirts for the boys. I knew right off they weren't going to like those stiff collars. "Come here," said Aunt Margaret, motioning to them. "I want to check the fit." Willy frowned and squirmed as she held the pants and jacket up to him. She nodded her head in satisfaction. "These should do nicely."

The last package contained piece goods—lengths of blue and green, a calico print, and lace for trimming. I stared in awe. She looked to have bought out the store. "It's high time you girls had new dresses. The ones you've been wearing are either shamefully short and tight or mended and patched till you look like a couple of street urchins. I trust your mother taught you some dressmaking skills."

Did she plan for us to make our own dresses? No matter. I was sure I could manage. We hugged and thanked her.

"You're quite welcome," she said stiffly. "I certainly don't want you running around in rags." I don't believe Aunt Margaret was used to affection. Hugging her was like hugging a post.

As we stood by the table admiring the purchases, Pa came in carrying pantry supplies. "Looks as though you children have done a good day's work," he said, sounding puzzled. "I didn't expect you'd have time to pick a wagon load of corn."

Willy was quick to explain. "We didn't do the picking. The Indians did! They were going to steal the wagon and all, but Hannah tricked 'em."

"Indians?" Pa put his arm-load of supplies down with a thud. "What Indians? Will someone please tell me what happened today." We all started in, but Pa stopped us. "One at a time." He looked at me. "You first."

When the story was told, Pa slowly shook his head. "Well, that was quite an escapade. You took a dangerous risk, Hannah. I'm just thankful you're all safe." You'd have thought he'd be grateful that I'd saved the corn and melons, not to mention the wagon! If he was beholden to me, I wished he'd come right out and say so.

Aunt Margaret had interrupted the telling repeatedly to exclaim, "Well, I never!" I think she was most shocked to learn that I had ridden out of the yard wearing Pa's overalls.

At the end of July, Pa made arrangements to take a load of produce to Brockton. I could scarcely wait, for I was going to Black Creek Canyon with Charles and Eliza. Aunt Margaret said she didn't fancy spending another day in a wagon. Indians or no Indians, she'd stay at the farm. She wasn't one to change her mind, so Pa didn't argue with her. He must have reckoned she'd be safe, since she'd been staying home alone every Sunday.

We left early the next morning soon as the cows were milked. It hadn't cooled off much during the night, but we'd be there before the sun had a chance to beat down on us. Dust billowed up behind the wagon as we rolled down the dry track past stretches of desert whose beauty had faded. Weeks had passed with nary a sprinkle of rain.

It was around seven o'clock when we turned into the lane at the Whitlock farm. Eliza opened the door, leaped off the porch, and ran to greet us. "Charles is near finished with his chores," she called. "And I've got the picnic lunch ready."

"I want to go on a picnic," said Willy.

"You're going to stay here with me," Nellie told him. "Annie Thornton's bringing Sarah over. Daniel Clement's coming, too. When Pa gets back from the market, we'll have our own picnic—with watermelon."

Eliza smiled down at Willy. "When you see the surprise Charles has for you, you'll want to stay right here. Let's see if he's in the barn." We found Charles forking hay down from the loft. When he saw us, he stopped and waved.

"Willy's come to see what you've got for him," said Eliza.

"Don't rightly know if Willy'd be interested." Charles climbed down and put his hand on Willy's shoulder. "But we may as well take a look."

As we walked around the barn, Willy stopped, then took off running. "Puppies!" he yelled. "I hear puppies." Who could mistake the high-pitched yipping and barking?

Inside a pen, round furry bodies tumbled and bumbled over each other as they scrambled to see us.

"Do you think you might want one?" asked Charles. "You get first pick."

Willy was speechless, but his head went up and down like a chicken pecking for feed. Charles opened the gate for Willy. As he knelt down, the six wriggling pups jumped all over him. You'd think it was a contest to see who could get in the most licks.

"Which one will it be?" asked Charles.

He patted and held them, giggling as they licked his hands and face. It took him a good while to decide, but finally he said, "I'll take this brown and white one with big ears. I'm gonna call him Patch."

Pa met us as we walked back to the house. Willy ran toward him yelling, "Pa, I got me a dog! Charles let me have first pick. Come see."

"That was right nice of Charles," he said as he put an arm around Willy's shoulder. "I hope you thanked him. It will be good to have a dog around the farm. I'll see him when I get back from town. I won't be long." He turned to me. "Be sure you're back here by four. We'll need to be home in time for milking. Your aunt might make preserves, but she would never milk the cows." Then Pa left to take his fruit and corn to the market.

Half an hour later, Eliza, Charles, and I rode out of Brockton past the livery stable. I willed myself not to look, but my eyes were drawn toward it. A shiver ran through me. I turned away, fighting off the memory of what I'd seen there. Charles rode up beside me, reached over and touched my hand. I decided right then and there that I'd never meet a boy I'd like as much as Charles Whitlock—even if he did have those fascinating brown eyes, dark hair, and crooked smile.

Chapter 18

Clouds lined the northern horizon as we followed the road to the Virgin River, shallow and murky with red silt. Soon we entered a narrow canyon cut into towering cliffs of red and gray rock. High above, a pair of hawks glided the air currents. As we wove our way along the river bank between straggly cotton-woods and willows, it was quiet except for the chirring of unseen insects and the clopping of our horses' hooves.

"There's a meadow about five miles ahead," said Charles. "We'll leave the horses there, then cross the river so's we can get to the mouth of Black Creek. I reckon it's a mile hike to the mouth and two more to the falls. Good thing you wore your sturdy shoes."

"Don't worry none about us," said Eliza. "I reckon we won't have any trouble keeping up."

I glanced down at my brown cotton dress, black stockings, and work shoes. They sure weren't much to look at. Too bad I couldn't have worn a pair of Pa's overalls. They'd make the hiking a good bit easier. I smiled at this outrageous thought. Of course, no respectable girl would wear men's trousers, as Aunt Margaret had made perfectly clear.

At the meadow, Charles hobbled the horses and led us along the river. How were we to cross it? It didn't seem likely there would be a bridge. Soon Charles stopped, and my question was answered as he said, "This looks to be a good place to ford."

Although the water didn't appear to be swift or deep, I wanted to turn and run, but there was no place to go. Panic bubbled up inside me and I felt sick. Eliza, showing no sign of concern, took off her shoes, tied the laces together, and hung them around her neck. Then hitching up her skirt, she waded out into the current.

"Come on, Hannah. The water's not deep," she called. As she moved toward the middle of the stream, I turned away and closed my eyes. Suddenly a scream echoed off the rock walls of the canyon. I looked back and she was gone. Seconds later she was floundering about in water up to her neck. My screams echoed along with hers. I grabbed Charles' arm and pointed, too frightened to speak. Then with a splash, Eliza rose up out of the river, laughing. Water streamed from her hair. Her dress was plastered to her body. The water came just above her knees.

"That was a mean trick," scolded Charles. But he laughed as he said it! Fear drained away, and I shook with anger. How could she do that to me? How could they laugh about it? Then I recalled they had no way of knowing about the childhood memory that had turned me into a coward.

"Come on," said Charles. "You can hold my hand. Water's not deep."

I'd made a dunce of myself. I didn't need his help. "I'm all right," I said. I hung my shoes around my neck same as Eliza had done, hiked up my skirt, and holding my breath, stepped into the river. I hoped my trembling leg would support me.

As I waded through the water Eliza called, "I didn't mean to scare you."

I managed a smile. "I should have know it was one of your jokes." Why did I have to be such a scaredy-cat? I felt foolish for making such a fuss.

As we continued up the canyon, each step was accompanied by the squish of Eliza's wet shoes. It served her right. She was lucky they hadn't floated away.

We followed the river where it ran close to the towering

rock wall, tripping over roots exposed by past floods. I shuddered to think what the river had looked like as it ripped the dirt away. Finally Charles stopped and pointed. "Black Creek's just ahead."

The box canyon looked like no more than a crack in the rock wall until we'd climbed past a rocky point. Then there it was. The shallow creek followed a boulder-strewn stream bed, tumbling over rocks covered with moss and lichen before emptying into the river. Steep walls rising on both sides were formed by jagged layers of rock, tan and shades of red and brown. There didn't look to be much walking room on either side of the creek bed.

"We'll stop and rest before we hike to the falls," said Charles. "Best keep your shoes on, Eliza. Wouldn't want 'em to stiffen up and shrink. I don't rightly think you could make it bare-foot."

We sat on a rock ledge while clouds from the north rolled across the sky. They'd been teasing us for the past week, as day after day we'd looked for rain to dampen the parched ground. "We better get going," said Charles. "Sure hope those aren't rain clouds."

"Doesn't seem likely. They look like the ones that blew over us yesterday without giving up one drop of moisture," said Eliza. I had to agree.

Before hiking far into the narrow box canyon, we were forced to scramble over large boulders and rock-falls while Black Creek burbled and splashed beside us. Protected by the high, steep cliffs, the narrow gorge was dim and cool. I had begun to think we would never get to the falls when Charles stopped and said, "Listen."

Over the sound of the creek came a louder splashing. We hiked past an outcropping of rock, and stopped, awed at what we saw. The hanging valley and falls were just as Charles had described them. Green plants clung to the cliff that formed the head of the canyon. Water poured through a crack near the top, cascaded down to a ledge, then splashed into a small pool before tumbling into the creek bed. "Isn't it something?" asked Charles. He set the pack of food down on a grassy spot near the pool just out of reach of the spray. Famished as I was after the hike, the bread, cheese, apples, and molasses cookies tasted like a feast.

After lunch, we took off our shoes and dipped our feet in the cool, clear pool. Tiny minnows darted for cover as we stirred the water, then swam back to nibble at our toes when we held them motionless. "It's a good thing your Aunt Margaret can't see you now," said Charles. "She'd think your behavior was disgraceful."

"Oh, I don't know," I said. "She might want to join us. She's growing right fond of the rinsing trough."

We sat by the pool talking about the summer and our plans for fall. When Eliza and I turned to talk of clothes and what we'd wear to the Harvest Dance, Charles lay back on the grass, then shot back up. "Sky's getting mighty dark to the northwest." As we followed his gaze, a spear of lightning cut across the dark clouds.

"Must be a good way off," said Eliza. "Can't hear any thunder." High above, billowing clouds scudded across the blue sky. The breeze picked up and grabbed at our hair and skirts. Across the northern horizon, sheet lightning flashed and danced against the gray sky.

"We better start down. Looks to be a thunder storm near the head waters of the river." Charles started packing up our things. "Come on, Eliza. Get your shoes on," he ordered, his words ringing with urgency.

"I'm looking to find my stocking. I don't see any call to rush. A little rain sure won't hurt us none."

"It's not a little rain worries me. Heavy rain upstream could be a heap of trouble."

He was right. Heavy rain up the canyon would send water rushing downstream. I crammed my feet into my shoes, not bothering to fasten the tops. We started down Black Creek, stumbling and sliding along the rocky bank. My skirt caught, and I heard a ripping sound, but paid it no mind. The water in the creek had begun to rise and was no longer clear but filled with silt and debris. My fear rose with the water. Clouds had settled overhead, and we could hear distant thunder.

"We've got to cross the creek and climb to high ground," yelled Charles. "Canyon walls on this side of the creek are too steep. There's a ledge at the top of a rock slide on the other side." He stepped out into the water and reached for my hand. I jerked away and shook my head.

"No, I can't!" I started to sob. I was trapped. I knew I couldn't stay here, but I couldn't force my self to step into the rushing water.

"Come on," urged Eliza. It's no deeper than what we waded through earlier. Just a mite swifter." She leaned out, gripped a boulder that poked out of the water and waded in.

Charles turned back and grabbed my arm. "Come on, Hannah! The longer you stand here, the deeper it's going to get. We don't have time for your blubbering."

Blubbering? How dare he talk to me like that! I stepped in, and the current snatched at my legs, knocking me off balance. My heart about leaped out of my chest. If it hadn't been for Charles' grip, I would have been swept down the creek.

"Here," he said, "bend over and grab onto the rocks. We can go from boulder to boulder. It's not far. I'll stay with you."

The rocks on the bottom of the creek bed were slippery with moss, but the ones protruding out of the water were rough, providing a hand hold. My heart pounded as we moved sideways like crabs going from rock to rock. My feet slipped out from under me, but I grasped hold of a boulder and pulled myself back up. With each move, I feared I'd lose my grip, and the water would sweep me away. What must have taken minutes seemed like hours. We climbed out on the far side where Eliza waited. Then Charles led us along the bank. Thank goodness we crossed when we did. What had been a shallow, tumbling stream, now overflowed its bed and lapped around our feet as we ran to the rock slide.

As we clawed our way up the steep incline, rain began to fall. Stones clattered down behind us, dislodged as we slipped and scrambled up the rocky slope. Charles reached the narrow ledge and pulled us up after him. Out of breath, we sat together and watched, stunned as the creek became a torrent. A wall of water sent logs and boulders bouncing and crashing down the narrow canyon. The ground we had been walking on had disappeared under the swirling water. Shuddering, I bent my head and covered my face.

Charles put his hand on my arm. "Didn't mean to yell at you, but I had to get you across before the flood hit. The look in your eyes—one would have thought you were facing the devil and all his demons."

I raised my head and looked at Charles. "If you hadn't got me riled up, I might have stood there till the flood swept me away."

Eliza wrapped an arm around my shoulder. "Must be something bad happened to make you so scared of the water," she murmured.

I nodded. I'd kept it inside for so long. It had been too painful to tell, but I owed them an explanation. My fear came near to getting us all killed.

"It happened on the bank of the Platte River," I said. "I was five, same age as Willy. I've lived the day over and over in my dreams. I'm beginning to wonder what's real and what's nightmare." I stopped and wiped away a tear. "Our wagon train was waiting to cross over. I can still see the river, wild and muddy from the spring runoff. Everyone was busy tying down trunks and barrels for the crossing. Sally Richmond and I wanted to see what was happening—so we walked to the river. Her brother saw us standing by the edge and yelled for us to get back." I paused, choking back a sob.

"You don't need to tell it," said Eliza.

"If I tell it, maybe I won't keep dreaming it." I took a shuddering breath and went on. "As Sally turned around, part of the bank began to crumble away. She tottered on the edge, reaching out to me. All I could do was stand there and watch as she tumbled backward and disappeared. I'll never forget the fear in her eyes. She was my friend—and I couldn't help her." I paused. Silent sobs shook my body. "I've never talked about it, but I can't get rid of the dreams and the fear."

Eliza had her arm around my shoulder. Charles reached over and held my hand. Neither of them said anything, but I felt comforted. We sat together on the ledge and watched the havoc below.

Chapter 19

While we crouched on the ledge, the sky grew black and the clouds opened up, pelting us with giant drops of rain. Jagged streaks of lightning shot across the sky as thunder cracked and rumbled, nearly shaking us off the mountain. The storm was furious, but lasted only a short while. Then the dark clouds parted, their anger spent, and a rainbow arched above the canyon. Once the flow subsided and Black Creek was reduced to a shallow, muddy stream, we climbed down the slide, and following Charles, picked our way down the canyon, crossing Black Creek on a log wedged there by the flood.

When we reached the point where it merged with the Virgin, I stared, shocked at what I saw. It was not the river I'd waded across earlier. It was swift and deep with brown foam swirling in the current. We couldn't cross it now. How long would we have to wait for the water to go down? I slogged along the bank through mire left by the flood, trying to shut out the sound of the river. Suddenly Eliza stopped, and I came near to bumping into her. "Listen!" she said.

All I could hear was the rushing water. Then above the roar, I heard someone calling. When we yelled back, a group of men galloped into sight and splashed across the river. Pa, Brother Whitlock, and two neighbors had come looking for us. I ran to Pa as he dismounted. He slowly shook his head as he helped me up on Dan's back. "Oh, Hannah," he said. "Thank the good Lord you're safe."

With my heart pounding, I wrapped my arms around his waist and pressed my face into his back. I couldn't bare to look as Dan carried us into the swollen river. With water washing over my legs, I held my breath and prayed he wouldn't stumble. Finally he carried us up onto the bank, and I could breathe again. "Pa," I whispered, "I'm so glad you came, but we'll be late for chores."

"Chores are taken care of," he answered. "Brother Clement's boys rode over to do the milking."

By the time our wagon jerked to a stop in front of the house, I could scarcely wait to crawl into bed, but Pa said it was only fitting that we kneel first and thank God for my safety. I don't know what prompted me, but I said that Charles should get some of the credit. I immediately regretted my words, expecting an angry response from Pa, but he looked at me with concern.

"God wasn't going to come down and pluck you out of the water," he said. "We pray for God's help and blessings, but some prayers can only be answered through those here on earth." I could feel my face redden at the chastising. I knelt, and we prayed.

Two days later, Pa was loading the wagon with produce, preparing to take it to the tithing storehouse. I walked out to ask him about the corn we were to trade for an Indian rug. As I came around the side of the barn, I heard Aunt Margaret mention my name. I slipped behind a stack of hay before they noticed me. I couldn't resist the temptation to listen.

". . . school in Boston would be the best thing for her. Hannah's never going to grow up to be a refined lady if she stays here! Chasing off mountain lions and Indians, wearing overalls, traipsing all over the countryside with that Whitlock boy. That's no way for a young lady to behave. I'm sure Caroline would want better for—"

Pa interrupted her. "Margaret, I know you mean well, but there's more to being a lady than wearing fancy clothes and attending school in Boston. Your offer is appreciated, but Hannah—" Pa paused as Nellie walked into the barn asking if they'd seen me. What was he about to say? I wished I could have heard more, but I figured I'd best get back to the house. Whatever Pa said, it put Aunt Margaret into quite a huff.

Nellie and I thought it wise to retreat to the spinning room where we labored over the precious piece goods Aunt Margaret had given us. With the Harvest Dance not far off, I wanted something new to wear. Dressmaking, however, was proving to be a most tedious job. Setting in sleeves was especially trouble-some. We'd picked out more stitches than we'd put in.

"It's mighty quiet, what with Willy and Pa gone to Brockton." Nellie squinted as she threaded her needle. "I wonder what's bothering Aunt Margaret. She looks like she bit into a green apple. She's not said more than a word since Pa left."

"Could be they had a disagreement," I answered. "Best we stay out of her way. If we go downstairs she's like to bite our heads off. The way she's carrying on, I hope we have some dishes left."

We bent over our work in quiet concentration. Then Nellie looked up. "I think Pa's taken a liking to Annie Thornton."

"She's a nice lady. Couldn't anyone help but like her." So I wasn't the *only* one who had noticed. Knowing Nellie, it wouldn't be long till she had a wedding planned.

She took a few stitches, then looked up again. "The other day while you were off with Charles and Eliza, Pa came back early for our picnic. I couldn't help but notice he spent a good deal of the time talking to Annie."

"He couldn't very well ignore her." I didn't say more, but where was Pa's loyalty to Ma? I couldn't get rid of my feeling of resentment. While I sat there stewing about it, Nellie inter-rupted my thoughts.

"Oh, I near forgot. Pa left fruit and corn for Wala-ho-na in the lean-to behind the barn. She's bringing a rug. It'll look right nice in the sitting room."

"And it will be one less rag rug we'll have to braid," I added.

We worked until the spinning room became uncomfortably warm. Then Nellie and I set our sewing aside and went downstairs. The kitchen was deserted and looked none the worse for all Aunt Margaret's banging about. Her door was closed, so I knocked. "Nellie and I are going out to the garden to get a melon and dig some potatoes and carrots for supper."

The bed creaked, the door opened, and Aunt Margaret appeared, holding a damp cloth to her forehead. "I can't be bothered about supper now. If I don't get over this headache, you girls will have to fix the evening meal. I would appreciate some quiet."

"Sorry you're not feeling well," I said. "Nellie and I'll fix supper." We walked down the lane and had just reached the melon patch when Caleb came running across the field, yelling like Black Hawk was after him. "Get the gun! The lion's after the sheep!" I turned and sprinted off to the house with Caleb trailing behind me. "Wait up," he yelled.

I was about to burst through the door when I remembered Aunt Margaret's headache. I moved quietly across the room and lifted the gun from the rack.

When I met Nellie and Caleb at the gate, he glared at me. "Gimme the gun! I aim on shootin' that old mountain cat."

I held firmly to the rifle. "Wait till we get there." I turned, and we ran back toward the field where the sheep were penned. I wasn't about to give him the gun. This was my chance to make up for the foolish decision that had cost Ruff his life.

"Dang blast it, Hannah. You . . . had yer chance. You can't shoot . . . worth beans when it matters!" Caleb was gasping for breath trying to keep up. He'd run a good ways before he got to the melon patch.

I slowed and turned back to him. "Don't worry yourself about who's to do the shooting. Best we see if the cat's still there. What happened, anyway?"

He didn't look pleased as he answered in gasps. "Finished the irrigating . . . Went 'n checked on the sheep. . . . Could hear them bleating . . . like the devil was after 'em. Figured it must be the cougar." He paused to catch his breath. "When I got to the field, the sheep were bunched up in the corner . . . bawling something fierce. Tag, good-for-nothing mutt, must've run off. I seen blood on the ground where the cat had dragged the sheep. Don't see how he got it over the fence, but there was blood on the other side. I looked up by the rocks and seen him. I aim to shoot 'im 'fore he gets away."

"Well, he's not going to sit there if he sees us coming. You sure where it was you saw him?" I asked. "We'd best get down wind and try to sneak up on him."

"He was by the dead tree, the one got split by lightning." Caleb spit on his fingers and held them up. "Doesn't appear to be much wind. I'd say it's blowing in our direction."

We left the road and made our way through dry grass and sagebrush toward the foothills. Under cover of junipers and mesquite bushes, we crept along a ridge overlooking the spot where Caleb had seen the lion. I prayed it wouldn't hear us as we edged closer to the dead tree. Suddenly Caleb stopped, motioned us back behind a rock and pointed. The tawny cat crouched there, ripping at the sheep's flesh. He looked thin, half-starved, not the ferocious beast I remembered.

Up on the mountain when Ruff had died, there was nothing I wanted more than to kill the cat. As we crouched behind the rock, I realized the hate was gone. Revenge wouldn't bring Ruff back, but the mountain lion had to die. We couldn't have it killing our sheep. I looked at Caleb, so anxious to prove himself. I handed him the gun. "Best you shoot," I whispered.

He nodded, took the rifle and sighted down the barrel. As

he squeezed the trigger, the shot echoed off the rocks. Caleb let out a whoop. "I got 'im! I got 'im! You shoulda give me the gun that first time he came around."

I should have. Now I'd be forced to endure weeks of bragging, but I could abide it. I put my hand on his shoulder to keep him from rushing to the cat. "That was a mighty good shot, but you better make sure he's dead before you try to skin him."

We walked cautiously over to the lion, sprawled there on top of the sheep's carcass. Caleb reached out with his foot and gave the cat a shove. Its head flopped to one side. "He's dead all right. Got 'im with one shot!"

Nellie hugged him. "Pa will be mighty pleased," she said.

I had the urge to hug him, too, but I held back. I didn't think he'd appreciate it. Right now, he felt like a man. "You did right well," I said.

"Think I'll skin 'im. The hide'll make a mighty nice rug." As he looked up at me and smiled, I had hope we'd be friends again. Nellie and I climbed back down the hill and walked to the house, leaving Caleb to take care of his trophy.

Chapter 20

The day's excitement was far from over. As we walked up the lane, a fearsome shriek pierced the air. Couldn't anyone but Aunt Margaret sound like that. Breaking into a run, we tore around the house and nearly crashed into Wala-ho-na. She pointed toward the sheep pen, her plump body shaking with laughter. "Skinny white squaw. No clothes. Sit where horses drink." Nellie and I looked at each other, then burst out laughing. It was cruel, considering Aunt Margaret already had a headache, but we were unable to suppress our laughter.

Wala-ho-na had gone by the time Aunt Margaret stormed into the house, wet strands of hair hanging around her face, lips pulled together in a tight line. "Has that savage left? She crept over while I was bathing and tore down the blanket. I've never been so humiliated in my life!"

Nellie spoke up without so much as a smile to betray her amusement. "Wala-ho-na's not a savage. She was bringing a rug to trade. I'm sure she didn't know you were in the trough."

This explanation did nothing to tame Aunt Margaret's anger, and she continued with her onslaught. "How could your father bring you to this uncivilized wilderness? It's a wonder any of you have survived. I shall never forgive him for bringing your mother to this desolate land, forcing her to live under these primitive conditions. Caroline was used to a better way of life. Now she's paid the price for his foolish belief that God would bless and protect his family. Where were those blessings when she was sick and suffering and in need of a doctor's care?"

Her words cut through me like a knife. She had no right to

say those things about Pa. When she paused, tears escaped from my eyes and words from my mouth. "Aunt Margaret, you didn't know Ma—not the Ma we knew. She loved the farm. She and Pa worked hard to make a good home for us. She was happy here. People die and we don't know why God takes them—and not just here. We've heard about all the death and suffering in the war—and the cholera in Boston. You have no right to blame Pa for Ma's death."

"That's quite enough, Hannah. I can see you've not been taught to respect your elders. I consider that worse than Caleb's deplorable language. By the way, where is Caleb? I've not seen him all day. Water needs to be brought in."

"He's off skinning the cougar," answered Nellie. "He killed it with one shot."

Aunt Margaret was more outraged than impressed. "And where is your father while his son is forced to deal with a mountain lion? I'll tell you. He's off giving away your food! It's wisdom to save for a rainy day. I just hope you don't end up starving because of his foolishness."

I couldn't keep still. I never seem able to. "When we ask God to bless the widows and orphans and feed the hungry, we can't expect Him to grow the food. We have to be willing to help."

Aunt Margaret stormed into her room and slammed the door. Nellie shook her head. "My land, Hannah, you're sounding a mighty lot like Pa." Then she came over and hugged me.

When Pa and Willy got back from Brockton, Nellie ran to meet them. "Pa, you'll never guess what happened." Before he had a chance to guess, she continued, "The mountain lion was after the sheep, and Caleb killed it. Got him with one shot!"

"Well, doesn't that beat all! That's mighty good news. Where is Caleb? I'd expect him to be here to tell about it."

"He's on the ridge above the sheep pen, skinning it," said Nellie.

"I knew Caleb could get that old lion!" Willy sighted down his arm. "*Pow! Pow!*"

Pa took Willy by the hand. "Let's go see if he's needing some help. Otherwise you and I may end up with all the chores." As they walked down the lane, I heard Pa say, "With one shot! That's quite something." I rolled my eyes. I'd be hearing about Caleb's heroics for a good long while.

Aunt Margaret joined us for supper but was unusually quiet. She said nothing of her encounter with Wala-ho-na, and Nellie and I were wise enough not to mention it. Caleb made up for Aunt Margaret's silence as he recounted again the story of the cougar. When he came to the part where I handed him the gun, he said, "Yeah, Hannah decided she'd best let me do the shootin' this time." Pa looked at me, and the corner of his mouth twitched. I took it to be the hint of a smile.

The next morning, I figured the least I could do was fix breakfast, what with the bad day Aunt Margaret had endured. I expected Caleb to grumble about the mush, but he sat down and ladled it into his bowl with nary a word of complaint. He added applesauce, poured on thick cream, and claimed it was mighty tasty. Getting the mountain lion had certainly improved his disposition.

As for Aunt Margaret, she was still in a fine pucker. Nellie and I washed the dishes while she gave the floor a beating with the broom. She swept the offending dirt out the door and closed it with a bang. I decided it was time to apologize. "Aunt Margaret, I'm sorry I sassed you. I always say more than I should."

"We're alike in that respect, Hannah. I was upset and failed to control my tongue."

"You had good reason to be vexed," I said.

"That doesn't excuse my conduct. It wasn't my place to criticize your father. I'll be leaving for Boston in two weeks. He said I needn't stay any longer, that you're capable of handling the household responsibilities. Of course, that means you and Nellie won't be going back east to school since your father needs you here. If circumstances should change, he said he'd leave the decision to you."

I didn't know what to say. Aunt Margaret opened the door to her room, then paused. "Before it gets unbearably hot upstairs, you'd be wise to finish your sewing." With that, she closed the door.

As we climbed the stairs Nellie said, "I can't believe Aunt Margaret's leaving. You think it's because of Wala-ho-na?"

"No. I reckon she has to get back before her school starts." It seemed likely she was leaving because of her discussion with Pa, but I didn't mention it. After all, I wasn't supposed to be listening.

An hour later, Nellie stood on a stool while I marked the hem of her new calico dress. "Stand up straight," I instructed. "You want the hem to be even, don't you? Won't take me but a minute to finish if you'll just stand still."

"I hope so. I'm beginning to think we'll never be done." Nellie took a deep breath which caused the hem to bob. "Sorry," she said. "You'll see how hard it is to stand still when I pin your hem."

I had chosen the green gingham for my dress, but it didn't fit like it should. When I climbed on the stool to have the hem marked, Nellie sighed and shook her head. "Maybe the sleeves are in backwards." I climbed down and started picking out stitches. I had about decided to wear one of my old dresses when Nellie suddenly put her sewing down. "I know what you could do! You could wear one of Ma's dresses. Ought to be one just about the right size."

We went to the corner of the attic, and when we opened the trunk, the fragrance of lavender filled the room. I half-expected to see Ma standing there. I wiped a tear from my cheek and put an arm around Nellie's shoulder. "I'd best not wear one of her dresses," I whispered. "It wouldn't be right."

"I bet Ma'd be pleased if you did." Nellie lifted out a jade green dress with a lace collar. "You'd look right nice in this one. Pa's home. Put it on, and we can show him."

"I don't know. He might not want us getting out Ma's things."

"Won't hurt to ask. And Ma sure enough wouldn't want her dresses wasting away in a trunk." Nellie was right about that. Ma couldn't stand wasting anything. I put on the dress and followed her down to the kitchen.

When Pa saw me, the color drained from his face. "What do you think you're doing? Take that dress off and put it back where you found it." He didn't raise his voice, but I heard the anger in it. I turned and ran up the stairs. From the top of the staircase, I could hear Nellie trying to tell him that Ma would want me to wear the dress. When I came back down, the night went on as though nothing had happened. All through supper, Caleb and Willy talked of nothing but the cougar, and what a fine rug it would make. After chores were finished, Pa read a chapter from Dickens and passages of scripture. We knelt in prayer, then climbed the stairs to bed. Nothing more was said about the dress.

Unable to sleep, I lay there haunted by my thoughts. When I closed my eyes, I could see the look on Pa's face when he turned and saw me wearing Ma's dress. Was the look anger—or pain? And the words I'd said to Aunt Margaret. Where had they come from? *"People we love die and we don't understand why—You have no right to blame Pa—"* I'd been blaming him for close to a year. And what did Aunt Margaret mean, *"If circumstances change?"* The words, the looks, the feelings swirled round and round in my brain. Pa had told Aunt Margaret I was needed. I wanted him to say he loved me.

It must have been well past midnight and sleep still wouldn't come. Then I heard the stairs creak. Pa wasn't sleeping either. I climbed out of bed and went to the window. The door squeaked on its hinges, then Pa came out, walked down the path, and disappeared into the night. It must have been an hour later when I heard the door open, and knew he was back.

I couldn't leave things as they were. I felt my way down the dark stairway to the kitchen. Must be I looked like a ghost coming down the stairs in my white nightgown. "Hannah? What are you doing up?" Pa asked, startled.

I walked over to him and touched his arm. "I'm sorry, Pa. I shouldn't have put on Ma's dress. I didn't mean to cause you pain."

He wrapped his arms around me and smoothed my hair. "It's all right. Don't cry. It just took me by surprise. You looked so much like your Ma. Nellie's right. Ma'd want you to wear her dress." I stood there with my head against his chest, his arms around me. Although he didn't say it, I knew he loved me.

Chapter 21

Fourteen days after her encounter with Wala-ho-na, Aunt Margaret was packed and ready to go. For Pa, living with her for the last two weeks must have been like living with a porcupine, for he was often the target of her sharp words. It was fairly peaceable for the rest of the family since her usual doses of advise and criticism were absent. She read to Willy and even helped me with the green gingham dress.

It was seven in the morning when we stood by the wagon to thank her and tell her goodbye. The trip to the stage stop in Brockton promised to be far from enjoyable. She would barely speak to Pa. On top of that, it was hot, and Aunt Margaret had already begun to sweat. Remembering her arrival, I ran to the house and brought a pillow for her sitting comfort. I gave her a last hug, then waved as the wagon rolled down the rutted road taking Aunt Margaret out of our lives.

By the end of August, it was unbearably hot and dry with just a scant trickle of water flowing in the creek and little more from the seep that provided water for the orchard. The flowers around the house had wilted in the blazing heat. Water that still flowed from the spring was needed in the vegetable patch. The only rain we'd had in more than a month had come close to drowning me. Even then, little had fallen in the valley.

Pa came in from the field wiping sweat from his brow. "If we don't get rain soon, the sorghum isn't going to make it. There's hardly enough water in the ditches to dampen the ground." I knew he was even more worried about the orchard. If he had to replant, it would take years to produce a crop of fruit. Had Aunt Margaret stayed, she'd be reminding us how foolish Pa had been to take food to the tithing storehouse. She had said it was wisdom to save for a rainy day. It wasn't a rainy day we worried about. It was drought.

Each night Pa gave thanks for our blessings and prayed for rain. Every morning Willy scanned the sky for clouds, but each day was blue and cloudless. One morning he sat at the table, rested his chin on his hands, and sighed. "It's taking God a mighty long time to send that rain." I had to agree. Looked as though everything would dry up and blow away before it came.

Even Nellie had lost her optimism. We were peeling potatoes for stew when she looked at me, a frown wrinkling her brow. "You don't think Aunt Margaret was right do you—about Pa giving away our food?"

"How can we expect to be blessed if we aren't willing to help others?" There I was, sounding like Pa again. Trouble was, I wasn't sure I believed it.

Then Nellie tilted her head, and I knew she had more on her mind. "You reckon Pa's thinking to marry Annie Thornton?" she asked.

"He hasn't let on to me. Of course if he is, he ponders so long before speaking his mind, she's like to find someone else before he tells her he's interested."

"I like her. She'd be a far better step-ma than Aunt Margaret."

"Pa was never going to marry Aunt Margaret!" I said, exasperated at Nellie's persistence. But she had put into words the question I'd been wondering about. Would Pa marry Annie Thornton? I was fond of her, but I didn't like the thought of someone taking Ma's place. Could that be what Aunt Margaret meant when she said, "if circumstances change?" Maybe Nellie was right and she had planned on marrying Pa. Perhaps that was why she'd left in a huff.

A week later, my nightmare returned. I was back on a muddy bank where churning foam surged down the river, thunder rumbled, and rain fell from a murky sky. Suddenly a resounding crack shook the house, and a brilliant flash lit the room. I sat up, my heart thudding against my ribs. The rumbling had been real. Nellie raised up on her elbows, then leaped out of bed.

"It's raining!" she shouted as she ran to the window. Thunder boomed, rattling the windows, as a bolt of lightning split the sky turning night to day. Rain pelted the roof while water streamed down the window pane.

As Willy stumbled from bed, Caleb joined us to rejoice over the storm. We rushed downstairs and found Pa standing in the rain, his face tilted to the sky murmuring a prayer of thanks. Water streamed off his dark hair and beard. And he was smiling—a smile I hadn't seen for a good long time. We ran to him and reveled together in the warm summer rain.

By morning, there was a steady drumming on the roof, and the yard was beginning to look like a lake. None of us minded the deluge, least of all Pa and the boys who cheerfully took care of the morning chores, slopping through puddles to do the milking, gather eggs, and care for the animals. I didn't even mind the mud. When Caleb came in for the noon meal, he insisted that the fields were definitely beginning to look green. Worry lines had disappeared from Pa's brow. I rejoiced with them, but an uneasy feeling grew as muddy water rose in the creek, inching near the top of the steep banks. What was the matter with me? We'd been praying for rain for weeks. The storm showed no sign of stopping as somber gray clouds hovered low in the sky. Why couldn't things even out? We always seemed to have too little or too much water.

The next day, rain was still pouring down. Around three,

Caleb rushed into the kitchen. "You seen Pa?" Before I had a chance to scold him about the mud he'd tracked in, he blurted out, "Water's running over the sides of the irrigating ditch. It's like to wash the crops away, dirt and all."

"He's gone to bring the sheep up from the pasture," I answered.

"Someone's gotta close the headgate. With Pa off with the sheep, I'll be needin' you to help me."

In order to drop the gate into place, we'd have to cross the creek on a narrow foot bridge. I stood by the door, frozen with fear.

"What ya standing there for? We gotta hurry. Water's rising fast!"

I tried not to think of the rushing water, and just called to Nellie. "Caleb and I are going down to lower the headgate. Take Willy and go get Pa! And mind you don't let Willy near the creek."

Rain streamed down our faces as we raced up the muddy road that followed the Santa Rosa. Scraggly cottonwoods grew along the banks, but through gaps in the trees I caught a glimpse of the churning water filled with silt and branches. Caleb turned onto a path that led to the bridge. It was built of three-foot lengths of board nailed across two sixteen-foot logs. I hated it even when the creek was low, for it bounced whenever I crossed it. Caleb took no mind and strode over as if it were solid ground. "Hurry up!" he ordered when I hesitated. "Top soil's washing away while you're standin' there."

Fear had robbed me of my voice. With heart pounding, I stepped onto the narrow bridge that quivered under my weight. As I moved across the slippery surface, spray flew up and splashed over my feet while the rain pelted me from above. When I stepped onto the sodden bank, Caleb was waiting for me, a look of disgust on his face. "Never saw anyone so scared of water as you. It's gonna take one of us on each side of the ditch to lower the gate. I'll take the other side."

I didn't argue as he crossed the ditch on a wobbly board. Seemed strange, taking orders from Caleb instead of giving them.

The headgate slid up and down between two pairs of posts, one pair on each side of the ditch, another of Pa's inventions. The gate had been left all the way up so water would flow into the ditch during the drought. With the creek high and water flooding the fields, we would have to remove the rods that locked the gate in place, then force it all the way down to stop the flow.

My hands shook as I struggled with the rusty rod. The raging creek was no more than a foot away. I gave a sharp tug, the rod popped out, and I slid toward the water. With knees trembling, I gripped the post for support.

"Crimeny, Hannah, watch what you're doing. I'm soaked now. Don't want to be jumping in the creek to save you." I said nothing, just glared at him as I stood there shaking, my tears mixing with the rain.

With the rods out, we pushed down on the top of the gate. It moved easily at first, then stopped, and though we pushed with all our strength, we couldn't move it.

"Water's pressing it against the posts. Sure wish Pa was here." With that, Caleb gripped the top and swung out onto the gate. With a rasping sound, it dropped, tumbling him into the creek. I screamed as he sank under the water, muddy and filled with debris. Then he sputtered to the surface, and with the current carrying him downstream, he kicked and paddled toward the bank. Thank goodness he could swim.

I stumbled through the brush calling his name. His answering cry led me downstream where I found him clinging to an overhanging branch fighting against the powerful current that tugged at him. I hurried toward him, then stopped and screamed, "*Caleb, look out!*"

My warning came too late. I watched in horror as a log carried along by the torrent swung around and hit him, knocking him under the water. For a moment, I stood paralyzed, reliving the terror of my nightmares. But I wouldn't stand and watch this time. I raced along the creek searching the water. When I saw his blue overalls, I ran past him and jumped. Swift, chest-deep water knocked me into the swirling foam. As I fought my way to the surface, I saw a dark head bob past. I lunged and caught hold of an overall strap. Then we were both swept along in the rushing current. "Please, God," I prayed. "Help us!"

I kicked and flailed with my free arm, willing us toward the bank. The water pulled us under, then popped us back up. I sputtered, shook the water out of my eyes, and grabbed a willow branch hanging out over the water. The sudden stop came near to wrenching my arm off. My hand stung as it slipped along the branch. Just as I was about to lose my grip, it swung us out of the current toward the bank. Gasping for breath, I hooked my arm over an exposed root and pulled Caleb's limp body close to the bank. As my arm tightened around his middle, he coughed, and creek water spurted from his mouth. Blood oozed from a bump on the side of his head, but he was breathing. I didn't know how long I'd be able to hang on.

"Oh, Pa, where are you?" I whispered. "Hurry, please hurry."

124

Chapter 22

It seemed like I'd been gripping the root for an eternity before I heard Pa calling to us. I saw the look of fear in his eyes as he reached down for Caleb. "He's breathing," I said, my voice trembling. "He's not dead."

Pa lifted him up, then took my hand and pulled me over the edge. Paying no mind to the mud, he knelt at Caleb's side and prayed. I looked at my brother's still form and couldn't stop shaking. Nellie stood and sobbed, her arm wrapped tightly around Willy. Then Pa picked Caleb up in his arms and turned to me. "Let's go home," he said. "You can tell me about it on the way."

It wasn't until we turned in at the gate that I realized it had stopped raining. As Pa laid Caleb on the cot in the sitting room and wrapped a quilt around him, he tried to sit up, then moaned and touched the bump on his head.

"You fell in the creek," said Pa. "Seems a floating log gave you a right hard knock on the head. You came mighty close to drowning. Hannah jumped in and saved you."

"Hannah?" Caleb turned to me, a puzzled expression on his face. "But she can't swim—won't hardly get near the water."

"Guess it's time I learned." Then I smiled at him. "Just lucky I'm such a fine big girl."

While the others fussed over Caleb, I went up to my room to change my clothes. I didn't go back down immediately for I had something I needed to do. When Ma died, I accused God of abandoning us, but whenever trouble came, I'd called for His help. He hadn't deserted me. I knelt by my bed to thank Him.

Caleb came to the table for supper, and judging by his

appetite, he would recover. While we ate, Pa told us the creek had flooded the pasture and washed away most of the sorghum and second crop of corn. "We'll get along," he said. "We'll just have to do with a little less molasses on our mush. We haven't lost anything that really matters."

After supper Nellie and I took care of Caleb's chores. Then Willy got out the checkers and let Caleb choose—black or red. Nellie curled up in the armchair with a book. I walked out onto the porch and breathed in the sweet smell of wet earth. A golden glow spread across the land as the sun poked through clouds on the western horizon. Soon the sky was awash with color, gold, orange, pink. I felt a need to walk down to Ma's grave. It was near to a year since she'd died.

As I climbed up the rise, I heard Pa's voice and hesitated. Who was he talking to? I knew I shouldn't spy on him, but I had to know who was there. I walked around a mesquite bush and stopped. Pa was sitting on the outcropping of rock under the honey locust tree and appeared to be alone. He looked up, saw me, and motioned for me to come sit by him.

"I was talking to your Ma," he said. "I've shared joy and sorrow with her for going on eighteen years. No reason to stop now."

I sat down by his side. "Late at night when you left the house, were you coming here? Mind, I wasn't spying, but there were times I couldn't sleep." He nodded.

"You pulled the weeds and put flowers on the graves," I said. "I thought it was Aunt Margaret."

He put his arm around my shoulder. "The flowers were your aunt's doing. She is a caring person, just has a hard time showing it. Guess the same could be said of me. It vexed her when I said it was best she go back to her teaching. She wasn't meant for farm life." He paused for a moment, then continued, "Your ma'd be right proud of you, the way you've taken over. I couldn't have gotten along without you. You took over the house and cared for Willy. I didn't seem able to comfort him like you could. And today, that was a brave thing you did, jumping into the water. I know how you feared it."

"I couldn't stand there while he drowned." I hesitated, then plunged ahead with the question I'd been wanting to ask. "Nellie and I've been wondering, are you thinking to marry Annie Thornton?"

He smiled. "It's early to say. She's a fine woman. I don't reckon your Ma would mind if I were to court her."

"If you marry her, would you send Nellie and me to Boston?"

"Would you want to go?"

"I thought once that I might, but the people I love are here."

We sat together looking out across the peaceful valley fresh from the rain. Then he sighed. "I've sorely missed your ma."

"At times I was afraid you didn't care," I whispered. The words could scarce get past the lump in my throat. "At the burying, Pa, everyone was sobbing. You didn't cry."

"Nor did you. You and I, Hannah, we don't always let our sorrows show. I was foolish to hide my feelings."

I threw my arms around him. "I love you, Pa." The cold knot in my chest dissolved, and I cried in his arms.

A week later we climbed into the wagon and drove to Brockton for the Harvest Dance. When the sun had fallen behind the hills, the warm night air was filled with the joyous sound of fiddle music. Lanterns flooded the social hall with soft yellow light and the faint scent of kerosene. Doors and windows were open, allowing in a welcome evening breeze. The Johnson brothers fiddled up a lively polka, while couples young and old took to the dance floor. The noise was considerable what with the boys wearing heavy boots. Even the girls' shoes were more serviceable than elegant. Charles walked up to me and took hold of my hand.

"Will you dance with me?" he asked with that crooked grin of his.

"I'd be delighted, Charles Whitlock," I said.

As I whirled across the floor wearing Ma's jade green dress, I saw Pa sitting on a bench talking to Annie Thornton. He smiled at me as I danced by. I couldn't imagine why it had bothered me to see them together earlier. Life was too good to feel unkindly toward anyone.

About the Author

Shirley Rees was born in Salt Lake City. She attended the University of Utah for three years, took a leave of absence to marry and raise six children, then returned to school and graduated from Brigham Young University with a degree in education. For eighteen years, she taught forth, fifth and sixth grade students in Salt Lake and then in Star Valley, Wyoming.

Shirley says, "While teaching, I fell in love with children's literature. When I retired, I knew I wanted to write for young people. This work was inspired by journals and family histories written by my pioneer ancestors who helped colonize Southern Utah—pioneers who went about their lives with faith and courage. My aunt sent me a detailed description of her grandfather's farm. The farm in this story is based on that description. Most of the characters and events, however, are fiction, as is the town of Brockton."

Shirley now lives with her husband and two cats in the quiet town of Bedford, Wyoming. Along with writing, she enjoys reading, genealogy, snorkeling vacations, football games, and visits with her children and grandchildren.

9 26575 76526 0